EIGHT SECONDS

EIGHT SECONDS

SECONDS

Jean Ferris

HARCOURT, INC.
San Diego   New York   London

www.harcourt.com

Library of Congress Cataloging-in-Publication Data
Ferris, Jean, 1939–
Eight seconds/by Jean Ferris.
p.   cm.
Summary: Eighteen-year-old John must confront his
own sexuality when he goes to rodeo school and finds
himself attracted to an older boy who is smart,
tough, complicated, gorgeous, and gay.
[1. Homosexuality—Fiction.   2. Prejudices—Fiction.
3. Rodeos—Fiction.]   I. Title: 8 seconds.   II. Title.
PZ7.F4174   Ei 2000
[Fic]—dc21   99-48796
ISBN 0-15-202367-4

The text was set in Simoncini Garamond.
Designed by Lori McThomas Buley
First edition
A C E G H F D B

Printed in the United States of America

Many thanks to
Gary Weatherford
for getting me thinking about rodeos
and
to Larry Dane Brimner
for helping me find the story in them

ONE

With "HONKY TONK NIGHTTIME MAN" BLARING from the radio, Bobby gunned the truck down the dark, empty highway, grinning in spite of the blood on his shirt. His nose seemed to be a shape that invited punching and that suited him. He fought with enthusiasm, the way he did everything else. Fighting was just another sport to him.

I had blood on my shirt, too, and my lip throbbed and pulsed and felt as big as a softball, but I wasn't grinning—and not just because it would have hurt. I never said so to Bobby, but I hated fighting. I understood about wanting to hit somebody, but I didn't understand about actually doing it. You almost always got hurt, and nothing really got solved. It was a dangerous waste of effort.

I still fought, when I couldn't get out of it, and I did it as hard as I could. You kind of have to if you don't want to get totally creamed. Around here getting in a fight now and then is part of the territory of being a guy—along with riding spirited horses, being able to castrate fifty calves in an afternoon, and burping the alphabet after chugging a long-neck beer. I like riding the horses. I can do the rest—and I do—but I don't call it a good time. Sometimes I wonder about myself.

My oldest sister, Marty, the one who thinks she knows everything because she majored in psychology in college, says every teenager feels like an outsider in some way—even ones who've lived in the same place all their lives, like I have, and who have all the friends they want, like I have, too. But she says it's worse for me because of the surgery I had when I was six and the year of school I missed because of it. If she's right, that makes it a big problem, because there's no way for me to outgrow something that's permanent. So I hope the heart thing isn't all of what makes me have that outsider feeling. Then maybe there'd be a way to cure it.

"Your mom's going to pitch a fit over that shirt," Bobby said.

"What else is new? But Dad won't mind. He'll want to hear all about it. What about *your* mom?" I asked Bobby.

"With three older brothers? Are you kidding? She's just glad I come home every night. And someday I guess I won't be doing that, either." He gave me a sidelong look. "How are you and Kelsey getting along?"

Now there was a good question. I'd been going out with Kelsey for almost six months, since New Year's Eve. I knew there were a lot of guys who envied me. Kelsey was nice. And pretty, but in a way that didn't make me feel stupid and tongue-tied. We had a good time, and we never got in arguments. But I knew she liked me more than I liked her. That's not the most comfortable situation. Even when she wasn't touching me—which wasn't often—I could feel the pressure of her *wanting*. Wanting me to be more attentive. Wanting me to like her more. Wanting me to talk about a future. A future! I'd just turned eighteen and had another year of high school. All I was really sure I wanted in my future was more time with horses.

"We're doing OK," I told Bobby.

"You staying away from home nights?" he asked.

"If I was, do you think I'd tell you?"

"I can hope," he said, grinning. "But they don't call you Gentleman John for nothing. One of the reasons the ladies like you so much is they know you never talk."

"And that doesn't give the rest of you any ideas for success?" I asked.

"We can't all be such gentlemen," he said with a shrug. "It's way too demanding."

He stopped his truck on the road. It was a good walk down the driveway to the farmhouse, but his truck had a noisy muffler, and what was the point of waking everybody up?

"See you tomorrow," I said, getting out. "Hope your nose isn't busted."

"It's not," he said. "I know what that feels like, and this isn't it. I'm thinking about how Russ is going to look tomorrow at graduation with what I hope will be at least one shiner."

I shut the door as he said, "See ya, buddy," and drove off.

It was mid-June, after midnight, and the night was warm and soft, and heavy with the fragrance of sage. I stood in the driveway, looking up at that impossible river of stars, the Milky Way, wishing for...for something I couldn't describe. I felt nearly choked with anticipation, as if I was waiting for something big to happen, but I didn't know what it might be.

I went inside, pulling my shirt off as I climbed the stairs. I filled the sink with cold water—I'd had some experience with getting bloodstains out—put the shirt in to soak, and went to bed.

Clementine woke me early the next morning, jumping on my bed, the wet shirt in her hand.

"Oh, Johnny, were you in a fight?" she asked. "I took your shirt out of the sink and drained the water before Mommy could see it. The water was all bloody and yucky." She held out the wet shirt in front of my face. "But the spots came out, see?"

I pushed the shirt away. "Hey! You're getting me wet. Can't you see I'm trying to sleep?"

She straddled me and bounced on my stomach. "You have to get up now," she said. "I want to do the horses with you."

I groaned. Why couldn't she ignore me the way my other sisters did? Marty and Caroline were older than me, of course, and both out of the house—Caroline at college and Marty married and a mother already. I'm sure I didn't enter their minds even once a week. Sally was twelve and preoccupied with whatever odd stuff happens to girls at that age. But Clemmie was only six and I was her favorite toy.

"What do you want to help with?" I asked her, pulling one of her ponytails. "You want to muck out the stalls?"

She wrinkled her nose and shook her head.

"You want to brush and curry the horses?"

She shook her head again. "I want to give them the apples and the carrots and the sugar."

"You think they can take that from you without biting off your whole hand?" I asked, taking one of her hands and shaking it in front of her face. "This little thing? It's not even as big as an apple."

She giggled. "They never bite *you*," she said.

"How do you know?" I asked her. "They chase me around all the time, trying to take a chunk out of the seat of my pants. They're vicious, those old ponies."

"No," she said, bouncing on me again, chortling. "They're sweeties. I love them."

"OK," I said, pushing myself into a sitting position and rearranging Clemmie. "I'm not going to be sleeping anymore, I can see that."

"Oooh, look at your lip," she said. "Does it hurt?"

"No, it feels great. I bet it looks good, too. That lopsided, bulbous look is so irresistible to the ladies, don't you think? The girls won't be able to leave me alone."

Clemmie fell over onto her side, the wet shirt making soggy splotches on the sheets. "I already can't leave you alone," she said. "I don't want you to have any other girls."

"Even Kelsey? I thought you liked Kelsey."

"She's OK," Clemmie said. "But you still like me best, right?"

I poked her in the stomach. "Right. Now get out of here so I can get dressed. And leave that shirt here. I'll hang it on the windowsill until it's dry, and then I'll put it in the hamper. Our secret, right?"

"OK," she said, jumping down off the bed. "As long as you let me do the horses with you. So hurry up."

"Boy, you're bossy," I said as she left the room. "And shut the door," I yelled. She came back and slammed the door, sticking her tongue out at me as she did.

I threw on boots, jeans, and a T-shirt and went downstairs. Through the kitchen window I could see Mom pinning towels to the clothesline. Far behind her, purple with distance, were the Rocky Mountains, whose size and grandeur Mom often invoked when she wanted to remind us of how insignificant we were.

Sally was leaning against the counter, spooning cereal slowly into her mouth while she turned the pages of a magazine laid out in front of her.

"Hi, Sal," I said, assembling my own milk, cereal, and fruit. "How's it going?"

She looked up, pushing her glasses higher onto her nose with a blue-nailed finger. "You got in a fight, didn't you?"

"It was for a good cause," I told her, slicing a peach into my cereal bowl.

"Really?" she asked, sounding interested. "What?"

"I was defending my good name."

"Oh," she said, turning back to her magazine. "That means Russ Millard called you a bad name. He does that to everybody. He's just like his father. Why do you think his mother left them *both* behind when she took off? It doesn't mean you have to get in a fight."

"Women never understand about fighting," I said, echoing my father and the male party line.

"Women are too smart," Sally said. She took her magazine and left the kitchen.

Russ Millard was a guy Marty could practice her psychology on. Big and good-looking, he lived with his big, good-looking father and grandfather. They seemed to be in a contest to see who could be the most narrow-minded, bigoted, and mouthy. Russ's mother took off when he was four or five. Marty could have some fun with Russ and his abandonment issues, attitudes toward women, and God-knows-what-else. No question, he was a certified mess, and not even the kind you could feel sorry for, because he was a mean mess. He was also a creative all-star name-caller. He never just called you a liar or a faggot or a coward. He'd call you a second-rate, lying sleazebag who wouldn't know the truth if it rode up on an elephant, or the prettiest butt hole in six counties, or so yellow, dandelions were jealous. But he never said it like it was a joke, which could make it a pleasure, even for me, to take a poke at him when he had made you his victim du jour.

Clemmie came bounding into the kitchen. "You ready?"

"Wait a sec. I want to finish my breakfast."

"I'll get the carrots and stuff." She rummaged in the refrigerator, filling a plastic bag.

"OK," I said, putting my bowl in the sink and grabbing my hat from the peg by the back door. "Let's go give them their picnic."

It cheered me up just walking toward the stables, toward healthy, uncomplicated horseflesh. The sun was already hot on my arms in a way that felt clean and simple. My dog, Howdy, came running from the stables and jumped, all four feet off the ground, onto me. No living creature has ever made me feel as valuable as Howdy has. The mere fact that I exist is money in the bank to him. I went down on one knee and hugged him, while he wagged and wriggled and licked my ear.

"Hey, Howdy, why don't you ever act like you're glad to see me, huh? Why are you so shy?" He grinned and licked me some more, then followed Clemmie and me to the stables.

There were four horses and a three-month-old foal in the stalls, none of them with any kind of impressive lineage. But all of them were American quarter horses—sturdy, smart, dependable, and tough. Perfect ranch working horses.

"Hi, Brownie; hi, Peaches; hi, Doc; hi, Jack," Clemmie said, going to stand in front of each horse as she greeted it. She put her arms around the foal's neck and rubbed her face on his cheek. "Hi, Windy. I brought treats for you-all. And then we're going for a ride. Aren't we, Johnny?"

"Sure," I told her. "I've got to make sure those repairs I made to the windmill motor are holding. And I want to check to see that there aren't any calves stuck down in that canyon bottom. Who should I saddle for you?"

"Peaches. You know I like Peaches best." She gave Peaches a carrot.

"OK, but first we work. You have to shovel, too."

"It's too yucky. I hate shoveling."

"No pay, no play. Just think of it as hay that's been run through a horse. Now help me get them out into the corral so we can clean up in here."

We were just finishing the shoveling, with Clemmie trying but being almost no help, when Mom came into the stable. The light from the open door behind her made her into a silhouette, and I could tell, just from the way she was standing, that she was upset. Sally and her big mouth.

"Good morning, John," she said. "I didn't hear you come in last night."

"Hi, Mom." I lurked in the shadows, hoping she wouldn't get a good look at my lip.

She stood quietly, her hands on her hips, for a while. Then she said, "Don't forget we're going to graduation tonight."

"I won't." Marty's husband's brother Beau was graduating, and Marty and her husband, Paul, were having a party for him and his classmates afterward at the old farmhouse they were restoring on the west edge of Paul's family's farm. Marty'd been on the phone with Mom every day about the arrangements. I couldn't see what was so hard about hot dogs and lemonade.

"I hope you'll behave yourself," Mom said.

"Sure," I said blandly. Mom had apparently never figured out that if you always expect the worst from somebody, that's often what you'll get.

She looked at me for a while longer and then went back to the house.

"She's mad," Clemmie said. "Could you tell?"

"Yeah, I could tell."

"You better be good tonight."

"Got it." Women. I swear. "Let's get this lime and straw down," I said to Clemmie, "so we can go. We'll see if we can find Dad and bring him back for lunch."

I couldn't wait to get on Doc and get going. Sometimes I felt like I wanted to ride off into another state. Maybe even another country, where nobody knew me, knew what I was supposed to be like, knew what buttons to push to get me going. Where I could be somebody else all the time. Or maybe just be the person I really was, without any sisters or parents or girlfriends pushing me to be what they wanted. Kelsey wanted me more involved with her, and Clemmie wanted me always available to *her*, and Mom couldn't seem to help expecting me to be a problem, and Dad couldn't seem to help encouraging me to be one.

I understood why Dad did it. When I'd had my heart surgery, I'd almost died more than once. Dad was so glad

I'd survived that he decided I should do just about anything I wanted, have every experience. Maybe he still expected me to die young and wanted me to pack everything in before I took that long dirt nap. Or maybe he saw everything I did as a celebration of life, an affirmation of health and normalcy.

Mom was just the opposite. She acted like getting my life saved had been a lot of trouble—especially with Sally just a new baby and two other kids to see to—and she didn't want me to turn out to be a bum. She took everything I did wrong as some sort of personal betrayal, even average teenage male behavior. She didn't seem impressed that I was known at school as Gentleman John. And she was pretty pissed at Dad, too, for having a different standard for me than he had for the girls.

Clemmie and I, with Howdy trotting behind us, rode out through the pasture where we'd put Jack and Brownie and her foal, Windy, to graze, and then we threaded our way along the path to the dirt road that ran between two fields of alfalfa. Doc was the opposite of me: serene, untroubled, placid. Not the most exciting horse to ride but just what I needed then.

After checking on the windmill motor and getting a couple of calves out of the canyon bottom, we found Dad in the north pasture, mending fences.

"Hey, cowboy," he said when he saw me.

"And cowgirl, too," Clemmie added. "Don't forget the cowgirl."

"Well hey, cowgirl, too," Dad said. He took his hat off, wiped his forehead with a big blue bandanna, and resettled his hat. "You guys come to get me for lunch? Can I hitch a ride with one of you so I don't have to bring the pickup in?"

"Me, me!" Clemmie said. "Peaches is bigger than Doc. She can take us both. Then I can bring you back after lunch."

"OK, cowgirl," Dad said, hauling himself up onto Peaches, behind Clemmie, letting his legs hang. We turned and walked the horses back toward the house, side by side, insects buzzing in the noontime heat, the dry smell of hot grasses all around us.

"I've been thinking, John," my dad said, "and I've got a surprise for you."

"You do? What is it?"

"Well, you know, we got some pretty good county fairs coming up this summer. Three counties are having centennials so their fairs'll be big deals, and then the state fair, which is always a big thing."

"Yeah?"

"It occurred to me," Dad went on, "that this year you might want to enter the rodeos in some of those fairs. There's good money to be won, and you're as fine a horseman as they come."

"But I don't know anything about rodeo events," I said, "except for the mutton busting I did when I was about eight."

"You've been on horses all your life," Dad said. "You've got guts and nerve. You're a natural. If you're interested, I'll send you to rodeo school to get you ready. It's only six days, but it's all rodeo, all the time."

"Holy buckets," I said. Six days away from everything familiar. Six days of riding.

"Does that mean you're interested?"

"Well, sure. I mean, who wouldn't be? When is it?"

"Week after next. Then it's just a week until the first county fair. You'd be all set."

I didn't know if I cared about actually being in a rodeo, but I did know I wanted some time off, time spent mostly with just animals. "Can I get in? It's kind of late."

"You're already in," Dad said. "I signed you up last week." He laughed when he saw my face. "I knew you'd want to do it. I was just waiting for a good time to tell you."

"Isn't it kind of expensive?" Money is always a problem for a ranching family, and it was more so now with Caro in college and me a year away from going.

"Don't worry about that," Dad said. "I've got it covered."

I hoped so. I didn't want to keep hearing about it from Mom. She thought Dad favored me over the girls, and she wasn't wrong. Not that he didn't love his daughters, but that son thing was a whole different ball game. I felt guilty about it sometimes, but when I tried to talk to Dad about it, he always said stuff like we guys had to stick together, and there were things men understood that women didn't. It was useless. And to be stone-cold honest, I liked the perks I got as the only son.

But I knew Mom wasn't going to be happy about the rodeo school. It had to cost *something,* which meant there was a trade-off for the girls, something extra they wouldn't be getting. Not to mention the load of my chores that someone else would have to shoulder while I was gone. And I knew Mom would think I was being rewarded just for being male.

I decided to let Dad tackle that problem. All I cared about right then was getting away.

Two

GRADUATION WAS AT SEVEN O'CLOCK, BUT THE SUN wasn't down yet and the feebly air-conditioned gym was an oven. I'd bet my week at rodeo school that most of the graduates weren't wearing much under their robes. I wouldn't have been.

In fact, I should have been graduating with this class, like Beau, Bobby, and Russ were doing. Except for my sick year, I would have been. Instead, I'd always been the oldest one in my class, and I never escaped the feeling of being in the wrong place—too big and too old for the class I was in, too far behind and too dumb for the class I should have been in. Bobby got points for never making a big deal of our different grade levels—and that was part of why he was still my best friend, the way he'd been almost since we were born.

Everything went OK except that Russ Millard, with one very nice black eye, let out some kind of rebel yell when he accepted his diploma, and Beau tripped on the hem of his robe going down the steps after he got his diploma and fell the rest of the way. We all had a good view of what he was wearing under his robe, and I was right, it wasn't much.

After, we trooped out to Marty's, and those daily phone calls to Mom had really paid off. There were little lights strung in the big old cottonwood trees, picnic tables covered with flowered tablecloths, washtubs full of ice and drinks, and a barbecue where Paul was cooking burgers and wieners, chicken, and corn in the husk. The night air was heated and gauzy, the sky, violet black and sprayed with stars. The heavy scent of honeysuckle from the trellis in back of the house competed with the cooking smells.

Kelsey was plastered to my side, clinging to my hand. "We'll be doing this next year," she whispered to me. "We'll be graduated and through with school and grown-up. We can do whatever we want." She squeezed my hand. "You know what I want?"

I was afraid to ask.

"I want," she went on, "for us to be together. For always."

Kelsey'd hinted before, but this was the strongest statement she'd ever made about *always*. She was waiting for me to say something, and there was nothing I felt like saying that she'd want to hear.

"Hey, John," Bobby said, coming up to us with a root beer in his hand, "have I got news for you."

"Yeah?" I said, more relieved at the interruption than I could ever let on. "What?"

"I'm going to rodeo school. My dad says he needs a break from me before I'm in his way for the rest of his life, and he's giving it to me for graduation."

"Well, how do you like that," I said. "I'm going, too."

"You're kidding me."

"Nope. My dad told me this afternoon. You think our dads have been talking?" It was possible. My dad was a very competitive guy, and if Mr. Bryant, Bobby's dad, had made a big production out of sending Bobby to rodeo school, my dad might have thought...But why try to figure it out? Bobby and I were going, and that was good enough for me.

"Who cares?" Bobby said. "Oh, man, this is great. It's great!"

Kelsey turned her face up to me. "You're going away? When? For how long? Why didn't you tell me?"

"Hey, Kels," I said, feeling guilty about how glad I would be to get away from her for a while, "it's just for six days. I was getting around to telling you. It's not that big a deal."

"Do you have to go?" she asked, still looking up at me, her eyes large and dark in the lacy leaf shadows.

"I *want* to go," I said.

"Uh, I think I'll go get a burger," Bobby said, backing away from us. "See you guys later."

"But what about me?" Kelsey asked. "What about *us*?"

"You're acting like I'm never coming back," I said. "It's just for a few days."

"But we've seen each other almost every day since we

started going together. I know I won't see as much of you now that school's out, so how can you think about going away from me? Especially after what we've just been talking about."

"Talking about?" I asked.

"You know," she said, squeezing my hand. "About being together for always."

"Well, I don't know about that," I said, feeling as if somehow all my clothes had gotten too tight. "Don't you think we're kind of young?"

"My folks were high school sweethearts. They got married right after graduation. I don't think eighteen's too young to be thinking about marriage. You'll be nineteen when we graduate."

I swallowed. "I don't know, Kelsey. I'll be going to college. I won't have a job."

"I could support us. You know I'm a hard worker. I'd make everything nice for you while you studied."

A barn rat in a rusty trap couldn't have felt any more panicky than I did. There wasn't any way out of this except straight through it. I took a deep breath.

"Kelsey," I said, "I like you a lot. You know that. But I'm not ready to even think about getting married. Not for a long time."

She was silent for a moment, and I could see the tremble in her chin, even with her face turned away from me. Then she turned back to me and said, "*How* long?"

Why was she doing this? Why didn't she get it? I didn't want to hurt her. I liked having her for a girlfriend. But I wasn't interested in anything more. Why couldn't she just be my girl for a while until we both grew up some more?

I took both her hands and pulled her away from the lights, deeper under the umbrella of trees at the edge of the party. I wished there was a way I didn't have to do this.

"Kelsey," I said, hearing my voice sound the way it did when I talked to Clemmie. "Kelsey. I don't think you should count on anything being for always with us." I could tell from the look on her face, even in the shadows, that I didn't need to say anything more. But I wanted to make sure she got it, and I was trying, stupidly, to soften the message. "I don't know if I ever want to get married, and I for sure don't want to think about it now. I figure I've got at least ten years before it might even be on my mind. You're a great person and I want us to be friends for a long time." I almost winced as those words left my mouth. I knew I would hate it if anybody said that to me. I could almost hear her thinking that if she was such a great person and such a good friend, well then, what was the problem?

And she would have a point. But I was going on pure gut instinct. I knew I didn't want a future with her, even if I couldn't say why.

"It's me," I went on, "not you. I'm an idiot, I guess, but that's how I am." I was babbling now, unable to shut up, making it worse by the second. "You're a terrific girl, and it's just the timing that's wrong." That wasn't true. No matter what time it was, I knew she wasn't what I wanted for always. "Maybe someday—"

Without a word, she turned and left me standing there. I sagged with relief. I would rather have had Russ Millard beat on me for an hour than ever do that again. Kelsey wouldn't be speaking to me all summer, I knew that for a dead certainty. Or at least not until she got a bigger, better, more devoted boyfriend—not until she could be condescending and superior and fully recovered would she give me the time of day. Thank God school was out. Thank God I would be going away for a while.

Marty came along with the baby in her arms. "Hi, Johnny," she said. "Having a good time?"

"Never better," I said.

"You sure?" She looked across to where Kelsey was standing alone, studying the diet Coke can in her hand as if it had the secrets of the universe written on it. "Everything OK with you and Kelsey?"

"Probably not," I admitted.

"She push a little too hard?"

Once in a while her psychology thing really seemed to work. "How did you know?"

"You're forgetting I'm an old married lady of twenty-four with a child of my own. I've lived through the Terrible Teens. And I must say, I'm not looking forward to doing it again with her," she said, nodding to the baby in her arms.

"Yeah, but you went with Paul the whole time. You had it smooth."

She laughed. "You were just a kid then. What did you know? He and I had one problem after another. We were trying to grow up together, and it wasn't so easy. There was a time, when we were seniors, that I was pushing him to get married. I didn't know what I wanted to do after graduation, and getting married seemed like an easy answer."

"So how come you didn't?"

"He wouldn't. He wanted to go to ag school, and he thought I should go to college, too. I concluded he just didn't love me. He and I broke up over that, and I didn't go out with him again until my junior year in college. But he was right."

"Yeah, well, I don't think that'll be happening with me and Kelsey."

"Don't be too sure."

I couldn't say how I knew, but I was sure. Her psychology machine was on the blink again. Now that my dorky, embarrassing performance of breaking up with Kelsey was over, all I was feeling was relief and sweet freedom.

There were times when I questioned if I'd ever be able to feel about someone the way Kelsey wanted me to feel about her. I'd never even come close, with her or any other girl. It made me wonder if my remodeled heart was capable of that trick, or if the surgeons had neglected to install some vital function that everyone else had.

"OK," I said, just to get Marty off the subject, to let her feel wise and experienced. "Maybe you're right."

"Darn right I'm right. Now come on out of hiding. Get something to eat. Talk to somebody else."

"Sure," I said. "I will. In a minute."

She went back to the party while I stayed in the dark beneath the trees. After a few minutes I inhaled, put my shoulders back, and went out to the party, acting like the Gentleman John that everyone was used to seeing.

I found Kelsey—and ignored the flash of hope that leapt into her eyes when I came up beside her and said her name.

"I just wondered if you wanted to go yet. I brought you and I won't leave you without a way home."

The light in her eyes went out. "Don't worry about me," she said without looking at me again. "I'll find a ride. You can leave if you want to. In fact, it might be a good idea."

It sounded like a good idea to me, too. I knew I should say good night to Marty and Paul, tell Mom or Dad that I was leaving, offer to give somebody or other a ride, but I didn't want to. I just wanted out of there. So I got into the old pickup Dad let me drive, and left.

For the next week I was the ideal person. I did my chores, I played with Clemmie and didn't bug Sally, I went into town with Bobby to the movies or to hang out at the Dairy Queen, but I kept my mouth shut and my hands in my pockets.

"Hey, man, what's wrong with you?" Bobby asked me. "You getting sick or something?"

"I'm OK."

"You're taking this breakup with Kelsey pretty hard,

aren't you? I don't blame you. She's hot. You sure it's too late to get her back?"

I'd let Bobby think that breaking up had been Kelsey's idea. All I said was that she'd decided it wasn't going to work out with us, and that we shouldn't waste any more time on it. All of that was true, technically.

"I don't think I want to talk about it anymore," I said, and changed the subject. "I didn't know you were interested in rodeo."

"Well, I never thought much about it," Bobby said, easily diverted to something that interested him more than my love life, or lack of one. "But I'm a natural for it. So are you. We were in saddles before we could walk. We've broken horses. We can rope and chase cows. How hard can it be? My dad says rodeos started with cowboys just showing off the stuff they did every day, anyway."

"What about the bull riding? Nobody was doing *that* every day."

"Yeah, what about that?" he said. "Do you have to be certifiable to do it, or what? It's supposed to be the most dangerous sport there is. More than auto racing or ski racing or skydiving. And you have to pay pretty good entry fees for the privilege of doing it. What a deal."

"You think you'd be interested in trying it?"

He didn't hesitate even an instant. I knew he wouldn't. Not Bobby. "Why not? You only have to stay aboard for eight seconds. That's not impossible."

"Probably seems like a very long eight seconds."

"Eight seconds is eight seconds," he said.

"You think so? Sitting on a hot stove for eight seconds probably feels a lot longer than kissing your favorite fantasy woman for eight seconds."

"Well, you're not going to be doing either, I don't think, so you might as well learn how to ride a bull."

The way I was feeling, it didn't even sound that hard.

THREE

CLEMMIE WOKE ME THE MORNING I WAS TO LEAVE FOR rodeo school. She sat on me and hit me in the head with a stuffed Shetland pony. "I don't want you to go," she said, bopping me. "Who will I play with? Who'll take me riding?"

"Ow. Play with Sally. Go—ow—riding with Dad. Or Mom. Take care of—ow—Peaches and Brownie and Windy. Hey, quit hitting me."

"Why do you have to go to dumb old rodeo school?"

"I *want* to go to rodeo school. Just like you want to go swimming at the municipal pool but don't get to go very often, so it's a big treat. This is my big treat. I don't want to swim at the muni pool, but I know you do, and I wouldn't try to stop you."

She threw herself off me and buried her face between my pillow and the stuffed pony.

I sat up. "You know, you're going to have to look out for Howdy for me. I need somebody who'll take really good care of him. You know how the other dogs sometimes want to fight with him and chase him. And he'll be missing me, so he'll need a lot of company."

She sat up. "Can he sleep with me?"

"You know Mom doesn't like that."

"But if you ask her. If you *tell* her he has to, then it'll be all right."

She was getting her revenge on me for leaving. She was maneuvering me to go up against Mom, something none of us liked to do because flexibility wasn't Mom's favorite thing. Once she decided how things were supposed to be, she liked them to stay that way.

"Clemmie, you know Howdy's used to sleeping on the utility porch. You'll confuse him."

"But he'll be lonely," she wheedled.

"Oh, OK," I said, deciding that was the only way to satisfy her. "But don't blame me if Mom says no."

I dawdled all I could while I showered, dressed, finished my packing, and had breakfast, hoping Bobby would arrive before I had time to talk to Mom. But Clemmie was at my side, harassing me the way the dogs did the stock; hurrying me, prodding me, badgering me until talking to Mom didn't seem like such a chore if it would just get Clemmie off my back.

I went outside, where Mom was trying to get her kitchen garden weeded and watered before it got too hot. Clemmie went with me.

"Hi," I said, and squatted beside Mom, pulling some weeds.

She squinted out from under the wide brim of the old straw hat she wore. "Hi. What time's Bobby coming?"

"Soon. Say, Clemmie's sent me to ask a special favor."

"Oh?" She shot a look at Clemmie, who was industriously picking at a scab on her knee.

"Ah...she's worried about Howdy being too lonesome while I'm gone. She wants to know if he can sleep with her."

Mom hadn't wanted me to keep Howdy when I first found him, a puppy abandoned by the side of the road in front of the ranch. People did that all the time. They'd drive out into the country and dump their unwanted puppies or kittens, sometimes sealed in plastic bags. We found a lot more dead ones than live ones. And when we did find live ones, Mom made us take them to the pound in town. A cattle dog, the kind we needed, had to have special talents and couldn't be just any old mutt from beside the road.

But Howdy was different. I knew it the minute I found him. He was in a plastic bag with his littermates, who were all dead. But not Howdy. When I tore open the bag he looked right at me and barked. He didn't whine or whimper. He barked, even if it was a weak little puppy bark. Like he knew it was polite to thank me and to say hello. That's why I named him Howdy. I could tell he was tough and patient, and a gentleman. And smart. I could see it in his eyes. I knew he was supposed to be my dog.

But when I brought him home, a double handful of curly white fur, Mom almost had a fit.

"That's a poodle or something," she said. "And a little one besides. He can't be a working dog, and you know we don't have room for pets who don't earn their keep around here. You'll have to take him into town, just like you've taken lots of others."

"I want to keep him," I told her. "I don't know why, but he's different. He can be a working dog. I'll teach him."

Mom had her ideas of how things should be. She'd been raised on a farm where every person and every animal had a place and a job, and that's the way she wanted it to be now. Fortunately my father walked in on this argument and put an end to it.

"Oh, Ev, what's the big deal? It's just a little dog. Let him keep it."

So Mom had never liked Howdy, even though he'd turned out to be as smart and as sweet natured as I'd known from the first that he would be, even though he never got any bigger than a water bucket and his curly white fur made him look like he should be a movie star's pet. To Mom he represented one more time when Dad had favored me.

"Please, Mommy," Clemmie said, in a tiny little voice.

"Howdy doesn't sleep in our beds," she said. "You'll only confuse him by letting him do it and then making him stop again when John gets back. He shouldn't have special favors any more than anybody else around here should."

I got the message. "Mom's right," I told Clemmie, standing up. I'd asked, like I said I would, but I wasn't going to the mat over this. Mom and I would definitely have other situations when winning would be more important to me. "I told you I'd ask, but she's right. You can spend all the time you want with Howdy outside of your bedroom. He'll love that."

I heard the sound of Bobby's muffler and the crunch of tires on the gravel drive, and was walking around the side of the house even before Bobby could honk the horn. Clemmie ran along with me, tears streaming down her face.

"Mommy's the meanest person in the world," she said, sobbing and hanging on to my hand. "She's so mean."

"She's just trying to do what she thinks is best," I said, barely even thinking about what I was saying. All I wanted to do was get in that truck and be out of here. No Clemmie, no Mom, no Dad, no Kelsey. I was tired of all of them.

I stopped at the porch where I'd left my bag. I knelt and hugged Clemmie. "I'm counting on you," I told her. "And so is Howdy." I tried to stand but she clung to my neck. "Clemmie, I have to go now. I'll bring you something special when I come back."

She raised her head. "What?"

"You'll see when I get home. Now, how can I go get it if you won't turn me loose?"

She unwound her arms. "OK," she said, sniffing hard. "I can be brave." Her voice had a martyred tone. "I'll mark off the days on the calendar."

Mom appeared then and took Clemmie by the hand.

"We'll find some fun things to do, too," she said. She gave me a one-armed hug. "Be careful."

"Right," I said, and got in the truck.

I waved to them through the back window and then turned to Bobby. "Go, go, go!" I yelled as we turned out of the driveway onto the highway. "Get me out of here!"

"Things going nicely at home, I take it?" he said.

"Women!" I said. "Between Kelsey, my sisters, and my mom, I've hardly had a peaceful minute in weeks. Do you think there'll be any girls at rodeo school?"

"Could be, for the barrel racing. But since that's the only event women can ride in, they'll have separate workshops, so it shouldn't be a problem. Don't worry, Gentleman John. It'll be a good week." He paused. "Except for one thing."

"What's that?"

"Russ Millard will be there, too."

"Are you kidding me?"

"Nope. It was a graduation present from his grandfather—who used to be a champion bull rider, wouldn't you know it. So I'm betting ole Russ is all pumped and ready to out-macho everybody else there. Good thing my nose has healed—I might have to be abusing it again soon."

I groaned. There went the vacation from my regular life. I'd accepted Bobby's presence at rodeo school—that was easy, even if it did mean less than a clean escape from reality. But Russ—he was excess baggage.

Bobby, who was never fazed by anything, said,

"Look at it this way. Maybe he'll break his neck falling off a bull or a bronc and go home in a bag."

"It's too much to hope for," I said, and turned on the radio, getting a nice comforting blast of John Conlee singing "Working Man" as we left our routines behind.

FOUR

A COUPLE OF HOURS LATER WE PULLED INTO THE DRIVE of the Tyler Thompson School of Rodeo, nestled in the foothills, looking out on a broad valley and back toward the rearing Rockies. From the look of things, the rodeo-school business was good. The main buildings, barns, and bunkhouses were freshly painted and in good repair. The paddocks, corrals, and pens were raked and watered, and the animals that we could see looked healthy and strong.

We parked in front of a building with OFFICE painted in fresh black paint on the front door and went in. Fifteen minutes later we were unloading our gear in a room with two sets of bunk beds.

"OK if I have the top bunk?" Bobby asked. "My brothers always take it at home, and I never get to sleep up top."

"Sure," I said.

There was gear on the other two bunks and on two of the four small dressers, but no other guys.

We'd been told to get unpacked and then to meet in the building next to the stables, where there was a class-room and a library, and where we would start acquainting ourselves with what we were going to be doing.

In the classroom a VCR played a tape of the 1989 Cheyenne Frontier Days Rodeo. Scattered around were piles of pamphlets and magazines about horse care, rodeo events, and rodeo stories. A couple of other guys—dressed as we were in Wranglers, boots, and long-sleeved shirts with pearl snaps—were sitting in the schoolroom chairs, watching the video and flipping through magazines. They looked up when we came in.

"Hey," Bobby said. "Bobby Bryant."

One of the guys, who looked familiar to me, stood up. "Hey. We're your roommates. I'm Kit Crowe and this is Matt Strauss."

When I heard Kit's name I remembered him from high school. He'd been a senior when I was in tenth grade. All I knew about him was that he'd played football, and that Caroline and all her friends had thought he was the cutest guy alive.

"I know you," Bobby said. "You were in my brother Doug's class at T. Jefferson High, right? Graduated last year?"

"Right, right," Kit said. "So you're Doug's little bro. What's he up to now?"

"He's at home, helping my dad. What are you doing?"

"I'm at State, hoping to go on to vet school."

"No kidding." Bobby sat down, already at home, effortlessly fitting in.

I stood, watching Bobby settle himself in, envying him his ease and straightforward friendliness, feeling, as I often did, that I didn't quite fit into the spaces available to me.

Matt was lanky and auburn haired, with almost no hips. Kit was taller than midheight, broad shouldered, and strong looking, but so were most guys who'd grown up on farms and ranches, hauling hay bales, muscling stock around, and spending more time on a horse than off. He was more than just sturdy, though; he was also perfectly proportioned. I couldn't really say how I understood that's what made him so striking: The differences between him and the rest of us were small, but evidently they mattered. Kit had exactly the right height for the leanness of his waist, for the ratio of leg to torso, for the breadth of his shoulders. Those differences, along with his clean-boned, gray-eyed face, made him so spectacular looking that it was difficult to take him seriously.

I know everybody wishes they could be really hot looking, but I've noticed that most hot-looking people are dismissed as being all surface and no substance. Or, as they say around here, all hat and no cattle. Sour grapes, maybe, but envy paired with fascination makes for some uncomfortable reactions.

Matt gestured to me. "Sit down. While you still can. I have a feeling we're going to want to eat our meals standing up after we've been pitched off horses and bulls for a couple of days."

"Thanks. Oh, I'm John Ritchie. Bobby and I came together."

"Ritchie?" Kit said. "You Caroline Ritchie's brother?"

"Yeah. She was in your class at T. Jefferson, too."

"And she's at State. I've seen her a couple of times around campus. But with twenty-four thousand students, we don't run into each other much."

"She wants to major in English, so you're probably not taking the same classes."

A man came striding into the classroom, followed by twenty or so guys between the ages of about sixteen and twenty-two. One of them was Russ Millard, traces of his shiner still visible. I could only be grateful for the fact that it was not his gear on one of the other bunks in my room.

"OK, friends," the man said, "I'm Tyler Thompson, and this is where we start learning about rodeo. Sit down and listen up."

He waited while everybody found a seat. Then he told us the story of rodeo; how it began with everyday cowboys competing with each other—showing off, really. The first rodeo to offer prize money was held in Pecos, Texas, in 1883, and the first to charge admission was in Prescott, Arizona, in 1888. Now the sport had grown so much that the prize money amounted to millions of dollars a year and a few top riders could make a very good living at it. Or, as Tyler put it, could make enough money to burn a wet elephant. But there weren't many of those. Most cowboys did it because they loved it, and their winnings could be measured more in friendships made and belt buckles won than in dollars. As Tyler said, "One day you eat chicken, the next day, feathers." And in rodeoing, you eat a lot of feathers.

Rodeo is a sport in which the cowboy must pay to play, and entry fees in professional rodeos are high. Neighborhood and nonofficial rodeos are different, and those—like the ones at our county fairs and even our state fair—were where we would likely be starting out. But the techniques we'd be learning would be the same ones we'd use even if we got to be superstars and competed only in rodeos sanctioned by the Professional Rodeo Cowboys Association. He told us rodeo was for people who were adrenaline addicted and able to play through pain, heal fast, remain mannerly in difficult circumstances, and remember to remove their hats only for the national anthem, the "Cowboy's Hymn," a beautiful woman, and certain types of brain surgery.

"You think you can remember all that?" he asked us.

"What about that pain part? And the healing fast part?" Bobby asked.

"There are a thousand ways you can get hurt rodeoing," Tyler said. "Not just by being stepped on or kicked by big animals, either. You can get a finger nipped off in a loop of rope pulled tight if you don't get your dally right. You can break bones flying off the back of a bronc and landing hard. While it's true that there's never a horse that can't be rode, it's also true that there's never a cowboy who can't be throwed. You can get smashed up in the bucking chute just waiting to go out and ride, if you've got a rank bull under you. I don't know one rodeo rider who hasn't broken at least four bones, and usually it's more. There's even one rider I know of who had his nose hooked off by a bull. As you know if you've been watching the video"—he gestured to the TV screen where the Cheyenne Frontier Days Rodeo still played with the sound off—"you can even get killed. Anybody want to go home now?"

Nobody moved.

"Good. I'm glad you're all ready to cowboy up. OK, first we're going to talk about safety. Then the fundamentals of each event. Some of you may already know if you want to specialize in one particular event—most cowboys pick a favorite and work on that alone. But there are some who compete in more than one event. Maybe this will help you decide. Then we'll go through the equipment."

"When do we get on the bulls?" Russ asked.

"You want to be a bull rider, son?" Tyler asked. "Why is that?"

"It's the toughest event," he said with a swagger in his voice. "And the biggest thrill."

"There're some who think that," Tyler acknowledged. "There are others who say that cowboys only ride bulls as an excuse to meet nurses. But I say the toughest event with the biggest thrill is the one you want the most to do, and the one that gives you the most satisfaction. There's body type to consider, too. Generally, bull riders are shorter than bronc riders. Steer wrestlers are heavier and stronger. Ropers are lankier. It doesn't mean you can't break type, but it probably means you'll do better at what you're shaped to do. You've got a bull rider's shape, son, so maybe that'll be for you. But we won't be getting on any animals until tomorrow afternoon, at the earliest. We've got lots of ground to cover first."

He wasn't kidding. We went through basic safety information, and we looked at safety equipment. Midriff supports and tail pads were getting to be standard equipment to protect ribs and rears. The assortment of knee braces, arm pads, ankle supports, shin guards, and sports tape could have been daunting if we'd thought we had a chance of getting banged up, but none of us actually believed it could happen to us. Somebody else, sure, but not us. Helmets, while probably a good idea, would never catch on with guys who revered their wide-brimmed hats and took pride in keeping their Resistols on through a whole eight-second ride and, if possible, even through a wreck that left them lying in the mud, with an excited bronc dancing around them.

I was getting on information overload pretty fast, so I was glad when we broke for lunch.

Bobby and I walked over to the mess hall with Matt and Kit. Just before we went inside, Russ came up behind me and pinched me hard on the back of my neck with his calloused hand.

"Howdy there, cowbaby," he said. "What do you think you're doing here?" He squeezed my neck harder.

I'd never been able to figure out how Russ decided who to single out for his attentions. He could ignore you for months and then spend a couple of weeks making your life hell for no known reason. Then, just as mysteriously, he'd go after somebody else and not even look in your direction. For me, watching him work somebody else over was almost as bad as having it done to me. I knew how it felt to have to go up against him when that was the last thing in the world you wanted to do.

I had to do something, so I tried to turn into him, but the grip he had on my neck made that impossible. I kicked backward with my booted foot, but I couldn't connect.

Suddenly, without my seeing what had happened, the grip on my neck was gone and Russ was lying in the dirt in front of the door, with the other guys stepping over him to go in to lunch. Kit was bending over him.

"Oops," Kit said. "Sorry. I guess I bumped into you. Can I help you up?" He put his hand out to Russ, who swatted it away.

"Keep your hands off me, you skim-milk cowboy," he said, getting up and brushing the dust off his pants. "And keep out of my way." Turning to me, he added, "Poor little yellow-assed cowbaby, can't even fight your own battles. Need a pretty boyfriend to watch out for you. Well, he can't be around all the time. And I'll be watching you."

"Such a big mouth," I said, ignoring the clench in my stomach. "Nothing but mouth."

"We'll see about that," he said, and, pushing past me, went into the dining room.

"Who was *that*?" Matt Strauss asked.

"A friend from home," Bobby said. "We're all very fond of him, even though he can be a mite touchy, as perhaps you noticed."

"He seems like a real sweetheart," Kit said. "Just a little rough around the edges."

"He's rough all the way to the middle," I said. I didn't think Kit understood what he'd started by tangling with Russ, and I didn't know how to warn him. Or if he needed warning. Maybe he was one of those, like Bobby, who enjoyed a good fight and sometimes went looking for one.

"Bull riders are usually gentlemen," Matt said. "They're tough enough that they don't have to be proving it all the time. Cocky is about as bad as they get. But then, we all have that problem."

"Cocky?" Kit asked. "Us? Us guys who think we're smarter and meaner and tougher than thousand-pound horses and one-ton bulls? You must be joking."

"Did you guys know each other before you got here?" I asked Kit and Matt.

"Nope," Matt said. "Just got assigned to the same room. But we both got here early, so we have a couple of hours' head start on the rest of you. I'm sure you'll be able to recognize that when we get aboard the beasts tomorrow."

Talking with his mouth full, the way he always did, Bobby said, "John and I've known each other since before we were born. 'Twins the easy way,' my mom calls us. You guys bull riders, too?"

"Not me," said Matt. "I haven't got the right body,

thank God. I'm more the roper type, I think. Anyway, I've had more experience at that, chasing down cows for my dad. What about you?"

"I'm thinking that's what I'd prefer, too," Bobby said. "But I'd still like to try at least one ride on a bull, even though I know ropers have to have real talent and bull riders just have to have big egos and small brains. Also, there's not as much chance of getting hurt in the timed events as in the rough-stock ones."

"Don't forget about humiliation," Kit reminded him. "I've seen some guys look pretty stupid when they've been outsmarted by a four-month-old calf."

"Yeah, there's that. Thanks for reminding me. Maybe I should have signed up for a week of sewing lessons instead of rodeo school."

"It's not too late," Matt said. "What about you, John?"

"Bulls. I've had a lobotomy already, so why not?" I don't know when I made that decision, but as soon as I said it, it felt right. I admit it was an odd choice for somebody who disliked fighting, since it had many of the same elements: the potential for getting hurt badly, the unpredictable outcome, the fear. But with the bull it was less personal, more sporting, and it had a time limit, which made it more interesting to me. How much could I do in eight seconds? How good could I be in that short time, against those big odds? And maybe there was something in there about proving that I was as tough as the toughest guys in spite of my worked-over heart and my reluctance about fighting.

Matt laughed. "Having a part of your brain removed is a real asset in a bull rider, I hear. Also saves having to do it later, after the bull steps on your head. Our pal Kit here, he's still got his whole brain, so he knows he's got time to change his mind."

"No way," he said. "We adrenaline junkies have a hard time finding fixes. Bulls are going to be mine."

We spent the afternoon in the classroom again, learning the fundamentals of each event. What looked simple and clear in diagrams and on videotape was likely going to seem impossible once we were on the backs of enraged animals. But at this point, we were all excited and optimistic and full of tough talk.

We went out to look at the animals we'd be working with the next day. Horses and steers were no mystery to any of us. We'd all been around them most of our lives. Even the testy ones didn't faze us. The calves for the ropers were no big deal, either. They were clueless little guys, kind of cute, bumping into each other, having no idea that tomorrow some cowpoke would be getting a rope around them, throwing them to the ground, and tying their feet together.

The bulls were another story. They were *huge*. Face-to-face with them, riding on one was no longer just a theory. And tomorrow it would doubtless be more real than I wanted to think about just then. At the same time, something exciting had hold of me—maybe it was that adrenaline need Kit had mentioned—and I could hardly wait.

"Which one do you like?" Kit asked me.

"All of them," I said.

Kit looked at me and grinned. "Yeah. Me, too. But I don't think any of them likes us."

"Not the smartest faces I've ever seen," I said.

"They're probably thinking the same thing about us."

"And they're likely right. No doubt looking forward to the fun they'll have tomorrow throwing us off their backs."

"No way," Kit said. "No way I'm leaving any bull's back tomorrow."

FIVE

KIT WAS WRONG. WE BOTH LEFT A BULL'S BACK SEVeral times, and in a big hurry, too. And it wasn't even a real bull—just a mechanical one. Classroom diagrams had no connection with what we were trying to do. Once I was on that contraption's back, my mind couldn't think of anything except trying to hang on. And with just one hand. Eight seconds had begun to seem like an unmeasurably long time. My longest stay on the back of the fake bull that first day turned out to be three seconds. And I couldn't believe it was only three. It seemed like an hour of getting my backbone slammed, my neck wrenched, my shoulder dislocated, and my posterior busted before I finally hit the ground.

Bobby lasted half the morning on the mechanical bull before he went to join the ropers.

"No challenge for me here," he said. "And my head's not quite swelled enough. You want to come with me?"

I didn't. In spite of the punishment I was taking, I knew this was what I wanted to do. Even having to listen to Russ brag and bray couldn't discourage me.

Kit and I limped in to dinner that night. Bobby and Matt were in slightly better shape than we were, and they'd been on real horses, working with real calves. But wrestling calves to the ground, even little ones, wasn't the easiest thing, especially when they didn't want to go down. And the whole debate was hard on the back and shoulder muscles of calves *and* cowboys.

Kit, Matt, Bobby, and I went through the food line, loaded up our trays, and then gingerly lowered ourselves into sitting positions at a table for four. I was shoveling in the macaroni and cheese when I heard a crash and Kit, sitting next to me, exclaimed, "Hey, watch it!" as he half rose from his seat. I turned around to see Russ standing behind Kit, Russ's tray dangling from one hand, a mess of broken dishes and spilled food on the floor.

"Oh, drat," he said with mock dismay. "What an unfortunate accident."

Kit was on his feet, too, with gravy down the back of his shirt. "What's your problem?" he said, putting his palm on Russ's chest and pushing him so hard that Russ took one step backward.

Russ dropped his tray and grabbed the front of Kit's shirt. "Don't you ever put your hands on me again unless you want that pretty face of yours messed up for good."

Kit brought his knee up between Russ's legs and Russ let go of Kit's shirt in a hurry. Russ doubled over, making the strangled sound we'd all made at one time or another, usually under more accidental circumstances. It isn't a sensation any guy looks forward to experiencing.

Russ was on the floor, both hands between his legs. Tyler Thompson and two of his instructors came on the run, shouldering through the crowd around Russ.

"What's going on here?" Tyler asked.

"Just a little accident," Kit said. "Russ here"—he gestured to the figure writhing on the floor—"spilled his dinner on me, and I guess I might have overreacted." He reached down and grabbed Russ's upper arm, pulling him into a sitting position. "He'll be OK. Won't you, buddy?"

Russ groaned and wrenched his arm away from Kit's grasp.

"Are you all right?" Tyler asked. "Do you want to see the doctor, Russ?"

Russ shook his head. I guess he figured he wouldn't enjoy having his privates manipulated any more than they already had been. "I'm OK," he grunted.

Tyler looked at him for another moment. "If you're sure," he said. Russ nodded.

"You'll be watching those overreactions, now, won't you?" Tyler said to Kit.

"Yes, sir," Kit said, and the two instructors went back to their own dinners.

Russ levered himself up. "We're not finished, doll face," he said to Kit as he headed off for another pass at the food line.

"I admire your guts," Bobby said to Kit. "Russ is a

difficult guy to have on your wrong side. He keeps coming back when you don't expect him."

"I won't start anything with him," Kit said quietly, "but once it's there, I'll take care of it." He sat back down to his dinner.

That was when I decided to take Kit seriously. He might look like he could be modeling for *GQ,* but looks weren't all there was to him.

After dinner we watched a movie called *Guts and Glory,* featuring the legendary rodeo stars Larry Mahan, Jim Shoulders, Casey Tibbs, and Roy Cooper, "the Super Looper." I was tired and sore, and wondered if I had what it took to be as good as I wanted to be.

The next morning, we hustled through breakfast, trying to pretend we weren't all hurting in a variety of strange places. Knowing that, thanks to Kit, Russ was sore in one place I wasn't was a good way to start the day.

We practiced on the mechanical bull again in the morning and finally got to the real ones in the afternoon. Naturally we were all jumped up and strung tight as we waited for our turns in the chute.

I know that when I'm trying too hard, when I'm too self-conscious about what I'm doing, I'm going to mess up more often than not. Striking just the right balance of making a maximum effort and being totally loose and focused on my performance is a very Zen state for me—which wasn't achievable that day, when I was hyperaware of watching myself like a bug under a microscope. I felt

Kit's scrutiny, too, and though it seemed to be just friendly interest, it distracted me. And that was even without the pressure of Tyler Thompson's eyes on me. And Russ's.

We'd been told we'd be starting on the gentler bulls, but when I saw the huge creature that waited for me, tossing his head, stamping his feet, and throwing himself against the sides of the chute, I wondered if there was such a thing. The idea of actually getting on him and trying to *stay* on by holding only a flat-braided rope that was merely wrapped around him and then around my hand, and that would fall off when I let go of it, seemed beyond ludicrous all the way to insane. It felt even more that way once I was on him, his broad back beneath my seat. Somehow I'd volunteered to ride a ton of explosives.

I can't even remember the ride; only the image of the ground coming up fast. But I was so protected by the thrill-seeking hormones barreling through my bloodstream, I didn't even hurt until hours later. On that bull I'd had a feeling of power—and of fear—that was the strongest emotion I'd ever felt. And I knew I wanted to feel it again.

When I made it to the rails, Kit joked that he'd seen a big poof in the dust when my breath had been knocked out of me. Later I was able to say the same thing to him. We grinned at each other like mental patients on a field trip, we were having such a good time.

I messed up over and over again, forgetting that I would be disqualified for touching myself, my mount, or my equipment with my free hand; forgetting to arch my back; forgetting to hold my chest high; forgetting to sit up on the rope. After dinner we'd be watching videos of our performances, and I knew that in the few seconds before I went sailing off the bulls, real and mechanical, I would look like Raggedy Andy flopping around. A demoralizing thought, but one that gave me a steely determination to cowboy up even more the next time I got on a bull.

Even though Kit couldn't stay on a bull more than three or four seconds either, he was the most stylish rider of all of us. Whatever it was about the way he was put together, he could hardly make a move that wasn't fluidly graceful, even if it didn't help him keep his seat any longer. I think we could all tell that if he could just master the techniques, he was going to have more point-winning style than any of us.

It didn't take long for Russ to start making fun of what he himself didn't have. "Hey, Kitster," he said, "you're in the wrong business. You should be taking up ballet dancing. You'd look pretty cute in a tutu."

"Hey, Kitty Kat," he yelled, "you might look good when you're falling, but cats don't always land on their feet. You're overdue for a big crash."

And again, "Hey, Alley Kat, aren't you afraid of getting dirty? Or messing up that pretty face?"

Kit seemed impervious to the taunting. And the instructor did nothing to stop it. I didn't know if he did nothing because he just didn't want to, or because he thought we should learn to perform under any kind of conditions. It probably didn't matter. But *I* wanted to strangle Russ with a bull rope.

As tired as I was that night, I couldn't sleep. I was sore and restless. I lay for a long time listening to the heavy conked-out breathing of the other guys while I flopped around trying to get comfortable and unconscious.

"John," a voice said in the darkness. At first I wasn't sure if I'd actually heard anything or if it was my exhausted imagination playing tricks.

"John," the voice said again, "are you awake?"

"Yeah," I said. "Who's that?"

"It's Kit," he whispered. "I can't sleep, either. You want to go outside for a while?"

"Sure." I slid out of bed, into jeans, T-shirt, and boots, and we eased out the door, though the way Matt and Bobby were crashed, we probably could have left with a marching band and not disturbed them.

We walked along the path to the arena and then hauled ourselves up onto the top rail. There was nothing to see except the silhouette of mountains, black against the dark sky. All the animals were in for the night, but we'd spent so much time there in the past couple of days, it seemed like a natural place to be.

The air was warm, the sky was clear and crazy with stars, and the whole place was sunk in a peaceful silence broken only by soft whiffles and foot movements from the animals in the barn and stables.

"Too sore to sleep?" I asked Kit.

"Yeah," he said. "How about you?"

"I'm sore in places I've never used before."

Then we just sat there, and the silence was OK. I was very conscious of him next to me, his arm braced on the top rail. I realized that I knew exactly what that arm looked like, even though I couldn't see it in the dark, from looking at it so much during the day. The space between his turned-back cuff and the edge of his glove was ribbed with muscles that stood out sharply as he held on to the bull rope. I glanced down at his arm and then quickly away.

He turned toward me in the dark, and I could see the pale oval of his face, his blond hair brightened by starlight, the white rectangle of his T-shirt.

I met his eyes for an instant before I looked away.

"Yeah," I said, suddenly feeling a need to say something to stop myself from thinking about his arm. "On those bulls today, that's a way I never felt before. Like I was being shot out of a cannon. It's nothing like riding the mechanical one."

"I know. We've got a mechanical one at home—my dad used to ride bulls when he was in college, and he never got over it—but this is the first time I've been on the genuine article."

"You liked it?"

"Yeah," he said quietly. "I liked it." He turned to me again. "It's an odd combination, isn't it—of working hard to use everything you've got, and also of totally giving yourself up to it."

He'd nailed perfectly the feeling of being on that

bull's back. "That's it," I said. "Control and surrender at the same time."

"I think the surrender part is harder than the control," he said.

"I think so, too."

We were quiet again, but something had happened between us: an understanding that hadn't been there a few minutes before.

"You have any brothers or sisters besides Caroline?" he asked after a while.

"No brothers. Three other sisters. Clementine's six; Sally's twelve; then me, then Caroline, then Marty. She's married."

"I've got one sister; older than me. She's getting her Ph.D. in psychology."

"Marty'd like to do that," I said. "She majored in psychology and she's always trying to figure people out."

"Yeah? What's she say about you?"

"Oh, she thinks I'm typical for my age. Insecure, alienated, confused."

"Is she wrong?"

I hesitated. "I guess not. But that's not all I am, either. Doesn't just about everybody feel insecure, alienated, and confused sometimes?" It occurred to me then that maybe somebody like Kit didn't ever feel that way. I wondered. "Don't you?"

"Do I ever," he said, and it sounded as if he was smiling when he said it. "But you're right, that's not all I am."

"What else is there?"

"Good question," he said. He looked up at the stars.

"Describing yourself is one of the toughest things there is. It's hard to think of three things to say about yourself—aside from insecure, alienated, and confused, I mean."

"You can't do it?" I was surprised. I could have said three things about him right off the top of my head: smart, tough, complicated. But he was right; I couldn't do the same thing for myself.

"Not fast. I'd have to think about it: What three words are the most me? How about you? Can you do it?"

"Not fast," I said. "How about *smart*?"

"Yeah," he said. "You're smart."

"Not me. I meant you."

"Oh." He was quiet for a moment. "I guess that's one of the words I'd have said. But it fits you, too."

"You think so?" I liked that.

The way I was talking to Kit wasn't a way I'd ever talked to Bobby, and he was my best friend. This was something new and personal and daring, like driving too fast on an unfamiliar road. Like getting on a bull's back.

"Tough," I added.

"You or me?"

"How about both of us?"

"OK. I think that fits. What else?"

"Your turn," I said.

He said nothing for a long time. And then: "Complicated."

"You or me?" I asked. This was too odd—all the same words I'd thought of about him.

"Both, don't you think?"

"Sure. Maybe we're twins, separated at birth."

"That must be it," he said. After a long pause, he asked, "You got a girlfriend?"

"No," I said. "Not anymore. Do you?"

"No. What happened to the one you had?"

"She wanted to get married. Can you believe it? I can barely manage myself. I don't know how she could think I was husband material."

"You miss her?"

"To tell the truth, I've hardly thought about her. Apparently she wasn't the right one."

"Guess not." He looked up at the night sky, and I could see the glint of starlight in his eyes. He took a long breath and let it out. "We ought to try to get some sleep. Those bulls tomorrow will really like it if we're too tired to get out of their way when they want to kick our brains in."

"Maybe we wouldn't miss them," I said. "They're nothing but trouble, right?"

"Right," he said, jumping down from the fence and dusting off the seat of his pants.

I followed him back to our room, but I don't think I slept at all for the rest of the night. I kept replaying our conversation and wondering why it had happened.

Six

I NEARLY DID GET MY BRAINS KICKED IN THE NEXT DAY. I was tired and my coordination was so off that it never did catch up with me.

Somehow interrupted sleep didn't seem to bother Kit. He was as cool and as competent as ever, and his technique improved with each ride.

By dinnertime I was wondering what I was doing wasting my time and my dad's money just so I could get thrown on my butt for hours at a time.

"How was your day?" Bobby asked me over the stew and biscuits.

"I'm lucky I'm not being kicked out for being terminally uncoordinated."

"I take it, then, that things didn't go so well?"

"I guess they went very well—from the bull's point of view," I said.

"You did fine," Kit put in. "So you had a rough day.

Tomorrow the bulls will be complaining over dinner about how they couldn't get you off them."

"Right," I said, discouraged. Turning to Bobby, I asked, "How's the roping going?"

"Good. Our instructor's got the right idea. He says if you're roping and you see your house is on fire, keep roping. It's more important."

After the videos, Matt, Bobby, and Kit stayed up playing poker on Kit's bunk, but I wanted that day to be finished. I was tired of thinking about my hopeless future as a bull rider. My personal lights were out the minute my head hit the pillow, and not even the racket of three guys playing cards could keep me awake.

I'd thought I'd need to be dynamited out of bed in time for breakfast, but I came suddenly awake at three in the morning with the sense that there was another wide-awake person in the room, too. I lay, listening. Bobby muttered in his sleep, words I couldn't understand, and Matt, above me across the way, breathed so heavily he could have been recorded for use in obscene phone calls.

"Kit?" I whispered.

"Yeah?" he answered instantly.

"You OK?"

"Yeah. I get insomnia sometimes, that's all. Did I wake you?"

"No. I don't know what did." I lay there for a while, as alert as if I'd been mainlining caffeine. "Kit?"

"Yeah?"

"You want to go outside?"

"Sure."

We dressed, then went to the arena again, where we took our places on the fence, watching nothing but the shadow of the mountains and savoring our memories of the previous day.

"You looked good out there yesterday," I said. I wasn't being polite. I'd watched him harder even than I'd wanted to, and could only admire his grace and strength and construction. I'd watched him in a way that I didn't think guys should watch each other, but I couldn't help it.

He shrugged. "Genetic luck. I'm put together in a way that works."

"More than luck," I said.

"I work hard, too," he said. "But having the right equipment's a big help. You've got it, too."

"Yeah? You think so? It sure didn't show yesterday."

"Yesterday was just practice," he said.

I liked knowing that he'd been watching me, too. And at the same time, it gave me an odd feeling.

We sat for a while in silence. And I, at least, was thinking about our conversation of the previous night. Without knowing I was going to say it, I told him, "I had heart surgery when I was a kid, and sometimes I think something got botched up in there."

He turned to look at me. "Physically, you mean? You think bull riding is dangerous for you?"

"No, not like that. The doctors say the operation was a total success, I've got a factory rebuilt model, lifetime guarantee. But it feels like something's missing, something I think other people have."

"What? What do you think other people have?"

"Something like...peacefulness. Steadiness. Sureness about what they're like and what they want."

"I don't think too many people have that," he said slowly. "But it's something probably everybody wants. Me, too."

"You've got it."

He turned to me. "It may look like that to you, but it doesn't feel that way on the inside. I'm struggling with it all the time."

"You mean, you feel like you don't fit in, too?" Kit, of anyone I knew, was the one I would have guessed had it all figured out.

He looked away from me, into the empty arena. "I'm as alienated as you are, remember?" he finally said.

We sat in silence on the fence rail for a long time. His arm was so close to mine, I could feel the animal heat of it. I wanted to touch the hot muscle of his forearm, the hard curve of his bicep.

After a while, without a word, as if we'd both heard the same silent signal, we got off the fence and went in to bed.

That day, in spite of my continued lack of sleep, I hit my stride. By then I was used to being sore, I'd had the rules drummed into me over and over, I'd done the right moves in my dreams—even if I couldn't do them awake—and my midnight talks with Kit had done something to me. Somehow it all came together when I got on my first bull of the day. I felt calm and clearheaded, even in the chute with the bull having a temper tantrum under me. Sure he was big, but so was a pickup truck, and I could handle one of those.

I cinched up the bull rope, wrapped the end of it around my gloved and rosined hand, wound it through my fingers, and pounded my other fist down on it to make sure the rope was tight enough. I was in such a trance of concentration, I could hardly hear the clanging of the bell hanging from the rope beneath the bull. When the chute opened, the bull exploded into the arena, coming down hard on his front hooves, kicking up his back ones, twisting in the middle. Somehow my body knew just what to do, even if my head wasn't quite keeping up. I found my balance point easily in spite of the bull's furious spinning, which formed the "well" that was so dangerous to fall into. I kept my free arm up and away, I raked his sides with my rounded spurs, and my hat even stayed on. I heard nothing—not the clang of the bull bell, not the yelling from the other guys, not the sound of the buzzer when my eight seconds were up. I was feeling like I could stay on that bull forever, until he got tired and I got bored. I finally came to, when the bullfighter hollered at me.

"Get off!" he yelled. "Give me a chance to do my job!"

At that, I let go of the bull rope, felt it fall away from the bull, heard the bell hit the ground, and I was in the air, off his back but not on my way into orbit. I actually landed on my feet, staggered some, and walked away as the bull took off after the clown and banged his horns against the barrel about a second after the guy had jumped inside it.

Tyler Thompson thumped me on the back as I climbed the arena fence. "You're going to enjoy watching *that* video tonight," he said. "Good job."

I came down on the other side of the fence, trying not to look as pleased—and as astonished—as I felt.

The other guys congratulated me, too. Knowing how the competitive male mind works, they were probably also thinking that they could outride me when their turns came.

Kit leaned on the fence next to me. "You made that look easy," he said.

"In a weird way, it was. Don't ask me why. Everything just worked the way it was supposed to."

"Feels good when that happens. Takes you by surprise."

"I'm trying not to forget it's a pretty rare thing."

"Maybe not. You might be the next Ty Murray."

"Don't bet any money on that," I said. "I just want to enjoy this feeling while I can—before the next bull freight-trains me and I have that old familiar I-don't-know-what-I'm-doing feeling again."

He nodded. "Yeah," he said.

We watched the other guys take their turns on the bulls. Something must have been in the air, because four of us made our first eight-second rides that morning, including Russ and Kit. We might all be learning how to hang on, but as for style, Kit was in a class by himself.

The perfect combination of power, coordination, and purpose.

At lunch Matt and Bobby were excited, too. Both of them had made their best roping times in the previous hour.

"What's going on?" Matt asked. "Did they give us power pills at breakfast? Have they sedated the animals?"

"Mine didn't seem sedated," Bobby said. "He was a feisty little critter. I just felt good, like I was finally getting what I'm supposed to do."

"Naw," Matt said. "Something's wrong. If it was really this easy, there'd be a lot more high-earning riders than there are."

"I just hope it lasts until tomorrow," Bobby said.

On our sixth day, the last day of school, we were going to have our own little rodeo so everyone could show off as much as he wanted. We would all get belt buckles, but the winners in each event would take home a big trophy. Everybody wanted one of those trophies.

We would have to wait for the fair rodeos to compete for the dinner-plate-sized belt buckles that the winning riders wore, decorated with images of bucking horses or bulls, fancy lettering, and, best of all, the word CHAMPION. We'd heard that those buckles were magnets for the opposite sex—buckle bunnies, if you wanted them, were part of winning.

"You guys are lucky," Kit said to Matt and Bobby. "You just have to be fast; it doesn't matter how you look. John and I have to do more than just stay on. We've got to look stylish while we're doing it. It's hard to look good while a bull's throwing you all around the compass."

He was wrong. At least about himself. Still, having one eight-second ride under our belts was making some of us feel pretty set up. And Russ was not an exception.

As he passed behind Kit, Matt, Bobby, and me, he gave us each a thump on the back of the head and kept going before we could react. We watched him do the same thing to a few other guys as he passed them.

"If he touches me again," Kit said in a low voice, "he won't be using that arm to hold on to a bull—or anything else—for a long time."

"Don't waste your energy on him," Bobby said. "He's just an ape-man. He's already forgotten he bopped us."

"I haven't forgotten," Kit said. "Once in a while, you have to draw rein on a bully."

Tyler Thompson was coming through the room, stopping to say a few words at each table he passed.

"How you boys doing?" he asked when he reached us.

"Fine," Bobby said. "Future champions, all of us. Don't doubt it for a second."

"I like to see you boys being good friends," he said. "Rodeo cowboys look out for each other, you know. They may be too proud to cut hay and not quite wild enough to eat it, but they take care of each other."

"Well, sure," Bobby said.

"But that doesn't mean they're not competitive."

"We're competitive," Bobby said. "Don't worry about that."

"That's good. I'm looking forward to watching you

ride tomorrow." He was looking at Kit when he said that. Then quickly he added, "All of you." But I understood what afterthoughts Matt, Bobby, and I were, compared to his pleasure in Kit's superior abilities. "Good luck," he said, and went off, stopping to talk to other boys as he made his way out of the dining room.

That night, I didn't sleep. I waited. Around three, with Matt and Bobby out cold, Kit whispered my name. We hardly had to speak before we were up, dressed, and headed for the arena.

We talked about our good day, our riding and how fast these few great days of rodeo school had gone, our love of animals and of this high, spare country. Our conversation never became as serious or as personal as it had the past two nights, yet I felt as if we shared a secret bond that I couldn't put into words.

Friendship is a mysterious thing, the way it begins and grows, and I knew I was learning a different kind of friendship with Kit, a deeper sort, one I hadn't had before with anyone else. There was a daring feeling to doing that, a sense of stepping into unexplored territory where something totally unexpected and new could happen. I wondered if this was connected to what I had been anticipating for so long, had felt so strongly that night I'd looked up at the stars and wanted something big to happen.

Bull riding is always the last event at a rodeo. Probably so no one will leave early. I don't like the idea, but I know there's something in people that makes them want to see somebody get hurt. Part of the reason, I guess, is that it makes the spectators feel lucky—and smart. They're probably thinking, *Well, at least I'm not stupid enough to have to ride a bull to earn a few bucks.* That's the reason trapeze acts are so popular in circuses, too. People don't watch them just to admire the performers' skills—they're secretly hoping somebody will fall.

For bull riders, even waiting for our event is part of what makes us think we're so tough: Trying to look cool and relaxed while we watch everybody else's wrecks and triumphs isn't the easiest thing.

I was the next-to-last rider, and when my turn finally came, Russ had already stayed on for eight seconds. His score wasn't that high because his style wasn't great, and his bull hadn't earned a lot of points, either, because he hadn't tried very hard to get Russ off. But an eight-second ride is an eight-second ride, and he still had the highest score so far. More than anything in the world, I wanted to outscore Russ.

Even in the chute my bull, Mixmaster, was wild. He threw himself against the slatted sides, bruising my legs and dislodging me from my carefully settled seat. I was glad for his bad attitude. A rank bull would earn more points than a sluggish one. When the gate opened, he exploded into the arena, coming down hard on his front hooves, then spinning in a tight circle, kicking his rear legs so high into the air, I had the sensation that I could see them just behind my ears. In three seconds I was on the ground and plenty grateful to be off his back. He came at me, his head lowered and his horns hooking for me. I rolled away from him and he missed me—but not by much. It pissed him off, too; he came after me again, his little eyes red and mean, his minute brain containing only one thought: my obliteration.

The clowns were dancing around him, flapping jackets and waving brooms, but he wasn't interested. I rolled, first this way, then that way, never having enough time to get to my feet and run before he was coming at me again. My heart was beating so hard I could barely breathe. My head was full of dust and noise and disbelief. Was I actually going to die today?

Finally one of the clowns blew a horn or a whistle or something, which made Mixmaster turn toward him, crazed with anger at a new source. I was able to get up and sprint for the fence—and only after I reached it did my legs start shaking so much that I needed help getting over the top.

"You OK, John?" Tyler Thompson asked me, putting a hand on my shoulder. "Things got a little Western out there, didn't they? Old Mixmaster sure is in a rotten mood. I think he needs to go to pasture for a while. My aim's to teach you, not to get you killed."

"I'm glad to hear that," I said, my voice breaking on the last word.

"You did fine, John," he went on. "You kept your head, you did what you could. You did fine."

"Thanks." All I wanted to do was to sit down and let

my adrenaline and my stomach get back where they belonged. "Maimed" could return to being a theoretical concept instead of a strong possibility.

Bobby climbed up next to me on the fence. "You OK?" he asked. "That old bull sure didn't like you."

"It's mutual," I said. "I'm just glad to have all my parts."

"Hey, Kit's up now, the last rider. I'd sure like to see him outride Russ if you couldn't do it."

Kit and his bull were out, the bull doing his best to get rid of the nuisance on his back. Kit rode as if he'd been born to it. His eight seconds passed in a kind of slow motion, giving me time to admire his technique and his style, the real beauty of the action between man and animal. None of us was surprised that he made his eight seconds and that he outscored Russ. Nobody, apparently, but Russ, who was the only bull rider not to come shake Kit's hand and offer congratulations.

At that night's dinner, Kit held his trophy over his head with the other winners—who included me, with my special trophy: MOST NARROWLY ESCAPING MUTILATION.

When dinner was over—and its speeches and awards and stories of the past few days—Bobby, Matt, Kit, and I made our way back to our bunkhouse with groups of other guys. We were feeling as tight as brothers, reluctant to give up our time together and the glamour of considering ourselves rodeo cowboys, reluctant to think about returning to the ordinariness at home. I knew I would especially miss those middle-of-the-night talks with Kit. We'd just gotten started with knowing each other, and I wasn't ready to quit.

"So when will we see you guys again?" Bobby asked. "You going to the Westin County Fair?"

"You know we are," Matt said. "I hope I can remember what to do when I have to go after that calf. I'll have to keep roping everything from the hay bales to my grandma to keep in practice."

"Come over and rope on our mechanical bull," Kit said. "I can make it buck hard enough to give you a workout."

"You've got a mechanical bull?" Matt asked.

"Yeah. It's my dad's—he used to ride real ones. He likes the fake one because he can control how hard it bucks. Control is something he's in favor of."

"How about it, John?" Bobby said to me. "We could go over for a little practice before the fair. Once or twice. What do you say?"

"Sure. That'd be good," I said, looking directly at Kit, into his gray eyes.

"It will be good," he said.

Seven

ALL THE WAY HOME THE NEXT DAY, BOBBY AND I talked about nothing but roping and bulls. We both understood how hard it would be once we were home, where nobody would be as interested in rodeo school as we were. Especially at my house, with so many women.

Caroline would be back from college by the time I got home, adding one more woman to the household. I'd be glad to see her, for sure. I got along better with her than I did with either Marty, who was always instructing me, or Sally, who was always annoying me. Or even Clemmie, who just didn't know when to quit. But Caro was still a female and she wouldn't get the fascination of bull riding.

As soon as Bobby dropped me off in my driveway, Howdy came flying across the yard and threw himself against me.

"You want to come in?" I asked Bobby, trying to postpone my full return to reality. I ruffled Howdy's ears while he tried to drown me with dog licks.

"Thanks," Bobby said, "but I better head on home. Can't put it off forever. I'll be calling you. We'll get over to Kit's for some more riding as soon as we can."

"Right. See you." I hefted my duffel bag and started up the porch steps, with Howdy glued to my leg. The screen door blew open and Clemmie was on me, almost knocking both me and Howdy down.

"Hi, Johnny! Hi! Hi! Hi!" she sang, her arms around my knees. "I'm so glad to see you."

"Clemmie, we're both going to fall down these steps if you don't take it easy."

She loosened her grip slightly. "I missed you so much. Did you bring me something like you said you would?"

"Bull flops," I said. "Flies. Busted bridles. All the fun things I had to play with."

"Really?" she asked, her voice sinking. "That's all?"

"No, that's not all," I said, taking pity on her. "I brought you a trophy I won. It's a little one, but I got it for escaping from a bull who was crazy and wanted to kill me." The more dramatic I made it sound, the better Clemmie was going to like it.

"He was crazy?" she asked, letting go of my legs and looking up at me with big eyes. "He tried to kill you?"

"Almost did, too. Would have, if a clown hadn't saved me."

"A clown?" she asked skeptically. "A real clown?"

"It's his job to get the bull away from the cowboy. It took him longer than I liked, but he did it."

"I bet you were scared, huh?" Clemmie said.

"Just about the scaredest I've ever been," I told her, picking up my bag.

"Caroline's home," Clemmie said, opening the screen door. Howdy ran in ahead of us.

"Yeah? How is she?"

"She's in love," Clemmie said, making it sound like "She has rabies."

"No kidding. With who?"

"His name's Ralph, but she says that doesn't bother her."

"I'm glad to hear it." I lugged my bag into the house and dropped it at the foot of the stairs.

"John?" Mom called from the kitchen. "Is that you?"

"Yep," I said. "All in one piece."

"Well, that's good," she said, coming into the hall, drying her hands on her apron. She pecked me on the cheek. "You want some lunch? The girls and I were about to sit down."

"Sure. Lunch sounds good."

Clemmie clung to my hand as we went into the kitchen. "Johnny brought me a trophy," she said. "Can I have it now?" she asked me.

"How about after lunch?" I asked, not wanting the first thing I did when I got home to be messing up Mom's lunch arrangements.

"I'd like it better now," Clemmie said. "OK, Mommy?" She knew who got the final say all right.

"It'll just take a second, Mom," I said, and went to rummage in my bag, Clemmie at my heels. I handed it to her and she ran back to the kitchen, carrying it.

"Look, look," she cried, holding up the little statue of a cowboy flying off a bull's back, connected only by his hand that wouldn't let go of the bull rope, "this is Johnny."

My mother took the trophy and read, "JOHN RITCHIE, MOST NARROWLY ESCAPING MUTILATION." She looked at me. "How narrowly?"

Clemmie grabbed the trophy back and put it by her plate.

"Not very," I said, minimizing my close shave, trying to avoid giving her any reason to object to my going to the county fair rodeos. "Hi, Sal. Hi, Caro," I said, changing the subject. "Welcome home." I sat down.

Howdy flopped at my feet, the place he knew he was supposed to be during meals, but he kept his eyes on me beseechingly, as he always did when food was in the vicinity.

Sally didn't even look up from her soup.

"You, too," Caroline said. "Sounds like you had fun."

"Avoiding mutilation may not be everyone's idea of fun, but it's mine. How was college?"

"Great. You'll like it."

"Yeah? Hey, I met a classmate of yours—from T. Jefferson, and from State, too." I dished myself up some vegetable soup and took a couple of ham sandwiches from the platter.

"You did? Who?"

"His name's Kit Crowe. He was the star at rodeo school. Looked like he'd been riding bulls all his life."

"Really?" She sounded surprised.

"Yeah, really. His dad rode bulls, and he's got a mechanical one at home, so Kit's had practice." Already I could feel the high of my rodeo school days leaking away. Nobody at the table cared anything about it. I might as well shut up right now.

"Huh," Caroline said. "I guess I'm surprised."

"Why? It's not *that* odd."

"Not because of the mechanical bull. Just that I wouldn't think somebody like him would be interested in rodeos."

" 'Somebody like him'? What do you mean, 'somebody like him'? He played football, didn't he?" I figured I knew Kit better than Caroline did—hey, I'd just spent a week sleeping in the same room with him, which I didn't think she'd ever done.

"I mean, I just thought he was more *political.* He's pretty active on campus." She gave Mom a sideways look. "In the Lambda Society," she added.

"Some fraternity?" I asked. "So why shouldn't he like rodeos?"

Caroline shot an uncomfortable glance at Clemmie. "It's not a fraternity. It's an, ah, interest group."

I waited. "Yeah?"

By now Sally was looking attentive, as was Mom.

Clemmie was oblivious, busy picking the peas out of her soup. We waited for Caroline to go on, our curiosity receptors at full extension.

"For, you know, people of a different"—she looked at Clemmie again—"persuasion."

"'Persuasion'?" I couldn't decipher her code.

"Oh," Sally said. "You mean he's gay?" She pushed her glasses up on her nose. Clemmie paid no attention, still after her peas.

"Well, that's who the Lambda Society is for," Caroline said.

Kit was *gay*?

"Shut your mouth, Johnny," Sally said. "I guess it wasn't obvious. Or else you're not very observant."

I shut my mouth and shook my head. I'd done plenty of observing of Kit. And I'd known something was happening with us, but now I saw everything about the past six days differently.

I felt like I'd been dropped on my head.

"People know about him?" I asked. "He doesn't care if they know?"

Caroline shrugged. "I guess not. He's out and active about . . . that issue, on campus."

"So does he have a"—I eyeballed Clemmie, who was looking from one to the other of us now, as if she'd finally tumbled to the fact that something was going on around her—"a special friend?"

"Of the male variety, you mean?" Caroline asked. "I wouldn't know. I don't know him that well. Though in high school I wanted to. He's so cute, and I had a major crush on him. I figured that the reason he didn't have a girlfriend was because none of us ordinary mortals was good enough for him."

So when he'd asked me if I had a girlfriend, was he really asking me something else? And why, when we'd been describing ourselves, was *gay* not a word he thought to mention? My stomach was in such turmoil I had to put the sandwich in my hand back on my plate.

"Can we talk about a more decent subject?" my mother said, her eye on Clemmie. This conversation definitely did not fall into her categories of appropriate table talk.

"If you want," Caroline said mildly. "But I don't see anything indecent about him. I just think it's a shame he's disappointed so many girls."

"Caroline," my mother said in warning.

"Who?" Clemmie asked.

"Just a guy at school," Caroline said.

"Ralph?" Clemmie asked.

Caroline smiled a secret little smile. "No, not Ralph. But Ralph is smart and nice-looking, too." Her smile got more secretive.

"Will he come to see you? Can I meet him?" Clemmie asked. Mom looked interested in the answer, too.

"I hope he can come," Caroline said. "He's going to summer school, but maybe he can come in August and go to the state fair with us."

"I thought you said he was smart," Clemmie said. "How come he has to go to summer school?"

"He *is* smart," Caroline told her. "He wants to graduate early so he can get into biz school early. He has big plans." She looked dreamy and smug, just packed full of little secrets. It was a way I knew I'd never looked about Kelsey.

"Where's Dad?" I asked. For some reason I wanted another male around just then.

"In town," Mom said. "He should be back soon."

I abandoned my sandwiches and stood up. "I need to go see the horses."

"Me, too," Clemmie said, guaranteeing I wouldn't have time to do any thinking. Good.

Clemmie and I were in the stables, Howdy at our sides, repairing tack when Dad got home. He whacked me on the back.

"Hey, son! How was rodeo school? Didn't break anything, did you?"

"No, but I almost got gored by a bull."

"Great!" he said. "Stuff like that makes a man out of you."

"It almost made a hamburger out of me."

Clemmie giggled, and Dad whacked me on the back again. "It's the bull who'll get to be the hamburger," he said. "Don't you forget it."

I had to tell about every minute of rodeo school— enough so that he could feel he'd been there, too—and I enjoyed the telling. He was interested in a way the females of the household would never be. The only part I left out was what Caro had told me about Kit. I didn't see how that had anything to do with rodeoing.

"Well, this Kit Crowe sounds like quite a guy," Dad

said. "I'll be looking for him at the Westin County Fair. He might have a future in rodeo."

"Maybe," I said. "But he wants to be a vet."

"Then I hope he gets a chance to work on some of the animals he rides. Give him a chance to get even."

That night I lay in bed thinking that only the night before I'd slept two arms' lengths away from Kit. I wondered if he'd felt attracted to any of the rest of us. If he had been, he was too cool to show it. But we'd all been attracted to him in one way or another. How could we not have found somebody like him magnetic? And if Caroline was any example, he had the same effect on girls.

Maybe Caroline had it wrong. Maybe she was thinking of somebody else, not Kit. Or maybe the Lambda Society wasn't really what she thought it was.

How could Kit be gay? Gay meant being a florist or a decorator; it meant wearing eye shadow and long scarves; it meant walking funny and throwing like a girl. It meant being somebody other people feared and hated and couldn't be friends with.

Didn't it?

EIGHT

THE NEXT DAY BOBBY CALLED, RARING TO MAKE A date for riding the mechanical bull at Kit's.

"I swear," he said, "I already feel like I never went to rodeo school, like it was a dream or a hallucination."

"I know what you mean. It doesn't take long for the old routine to knock the corners off the experience. You really want to go over to Kit's?"

"Well, sure. Why not? I thought you wanted to, too."

"Yeah, I do. You want to call him and set up a time?"

"Why don't you?" he said. "You know him better. And you're more suave on the phone than me, Gentleman John. Which reminds me, have you picked the young lady who'll be the lucky recipient of your attentions now that Kelsey's toast?"

"Give me a break," I said. "I'm still recovering."

"Well, you know the best cure for an old love. A new one. Not that I would know. That's something my grandfather always says to my brothers. And they listen. It's a regular revolving door of romance around here."

"Maybe you ought to join in," I said.

"I'm thinking about it. In fact, I wanted to ask you about something."

"Shoot."

"Would you mind if I—" He stopped. "I know this sounds bad, but—" He stopped again.

"You want to call Kelsey?" I asked.

"Well. Yeah."

"Why not? You might be just the right antidote to me."

"You sure?"

"Yeah, I'm sure. I've got no claim on her." I felt a small twinge of jealousy that vanished in a second. Maybe he *would* be just what she wanted—somebody completely different from me.

"Well, OK," Bobby said. "The worst she can do is say no, right? I'll call her, and you call Kit. Yours is easier."

I wasn't so sure about that. Before I could lose my nerve, I punched in Kit's number. I admit I was relieved when his mother answered and told me he'd have to call me back when he came in from helping his dad.

He called after dinner.

"You're lucky you got through," I told him, hoping my voice sounded normal, considering how squeezed my chest felt. "My sister Caroline's in love, and she and Ralph have been having these marathon phone conversations."

"Remember, I've got a sister, too," he said. "I know

how that can be. So, when are you and Bobby coming over to use the bull?"

"It's still OK?"

"Well, sure." He sounded puzzled. "Why wouldn't it be?"

"No reason...nothing," I stammered. "Is Saturday all right?"

"Saturday's fine. Come early and stay for lunch. Or come later and stay for dinner. Whatever."

"OK. We'll come early. See you Saturday."

Saturday was a good day. We rode the bull, we reminisced, we ate a lot. Kit was the same regular guy he'd been at rodeo school. I kept looking for a clue, a difference, but I saw nothing.

After lunch, while Bobby was on the bull, Kit turned to me. "What's wrong?" he asked.

"Wrong? What do you mean?"

"You're acting kind of...distracted. And you've been watching me like I've got spinach in my teeth or a third eye or something."

"I have? Sorry. I didn't notice..." But of course I knew exactly what he was talking about.

"You sure everything's OK?"

"Sure. Yeah. Fine. Everything's fine."

Before Kit could ask me anything else, Bobby got off the bull and it was my turn. When that round of rides was finished, I said to Bobby, "I think we ought to get going. I've got some stuff I need to do at home." Naturally, there were always things I could do at home, but mostly I wanted to get away from the strain of examining Kit, of waiting for him to somehow reveal himself. And of wondering what I would do if he did.

"So, I'll see you guys next weekend at the fair," Kit said.

"We'll be there," Bobby said. "And I've even got me a date for the barn dance Saturday night."

"Kelsey?" I asked him.

"Yeah. Can you believe it? Are you bringing somebody?"

"Not this time," I said. "I'm taking a break from women for a while." I didn't know why, but it made me uneasy to say that in front of Kit.

"You have a date?" Bobby asked him.

"No," Kit said. "I'm off women, too."

"Something bugging you?" Bobby asked me as we drove home.

"No. Why?"

He looked at me. "I don't know. You seem kind of . . . out there. You sure it's OK about me and Kelsey?"

"Of course I'm sure. It's nothing. I'm just thinking."

"I'll be good to her, if that's what you're worried about."

Bobby and I had cut our first teeth on each other. We'd ridden our first horse together. We'd been bitten by the same mean dog. He was the only brother I would ever have. But I'd never told him everything that was on my mind. There was a lot about me and my thoughts he would never know, and I didn't know why. I trusted him. I did. But there were things I was sure I was never going to talk to him about. Things I'd already begun to talk to Kit about.

And I knew I wasn't going to tell him about Kit.

When Bobby dropped me off at home, I waved and said, "See you at the fair." Then I went into the barn, saddled Doc, and took off before Clemmie could find out I was home and want to go with me.

We wandered, cutting along the edges of fields, crossing roads, skirting ponds. I didn't care where we went, so I let Doc find his own way. We couldn't get lost. From a lifetime of traveling through it, the whole county was as familiar to me as the barn at home. My head was busy with things besides directions.

I understood the utility of labels as a shortcut to knowing about people. If you called somebody a Republican or a librarian or a son of a bitch, you thought you knew them. But a Republican could have fantasies of monarchy, a librarian could have a wild side, a son of a bitch could love animals.

A label made you stop thinking.

I never wanted a label that would make somebody think they knew all about me. I'd just seen what labeling did to Kit—how it made Mom think he was indecent. But I'd known Kit before I'd known his label, and I saw how limited that label was, how irrelevant.

I pulled on the reins, halting Doc, who was happy to

stop for a snack of fresh summer weeds in the ditch by the side of the road. Did he care what label a boy on his back bore?

I decided suddenly that as soon as I got home I'd call Gwen Cassidy and ask her to go to the barn dance at the fair. Give myself another chance to get interested in a girl in a way I hadn't been able to do with Kelsey. Didn't Bobby say the best cure for an old love is a new one?

I jerked Doc's head up, and he turned to give me a wounded look before he plodded sullenly off in the direction of home.

NINE

I WAS JUMPY AND IRRITABLE THAT WEEK BEFORE THE Westin County Fair, and I wasn't sleeping much, but no one seemed to notice. Mom was baking one pecan pie after another, aiming for perfection and a blue ribbon. Sally arranged and rearranged her collection of miniature perfume bottles for the collectors' competition. Caroline spent her time either on the phone with Ralph or mooning about Ralph. Clemmie was satisfied as long as I let her follow me and Howdy everywhere we went, and sit on my stomach while she watched TV. And Dad, as always in this busy season, was too preoccupied to notice what anybody else was doing, though he did keep banging me on the back and telling me how much he was looking forward to watching me ride in the rodeo.

Early Saturday morning we were all in the van on our way to the fair. The final three pecan pies and Sally's collection were barricaded in the back, so well protected that a nuclear blast wouldn't have disturbed them. Marty,

Paul, and the baby were going to meet us at the picnic grounds at noon, the rodeo was at two, the dance started at seven, and the fireworks were at nine-thirty. In between those events, we'd be free to do whatever we wanted.

Once we'd parked in the dusty parking lot, Mom, Sally, and Clemmie went off to the home-arts exhibits, Dad to see the agricultural exhibits, and I to check out the animals in the pens behind the rodeo arena. I wanted to make sure Mixmaster wasn't among the assembled company.

I was leaning on a steel fence rail, wondering why bulls with no one on their backs seemed like nothing but big rectangular rocks, when somebody said, "Hey, John. How's it going?"

I turned around and there was Kit. In new Wranglers, white-and-blue-striped Western shirt, straw Resistol, and scuffed roping boots, he looked like a poster boy for rodeos: handsome, broad shouldered, all-American, and clean in thought, word, and deed.

"Hey," I said. "Which one of these do you want to do surgery on you?"

"None of them, actually. How come they look bigger than I remember from rodeo school?"

"Because the brain damage acquired at rodeo school has affected your memory?" I suggested.

"Maybe." He leaned on the fence next to me.

I was very conscious of how close his arm was to mine. I could remember exactly what that arm looked like when he had come out of the shower at rodeo school, a towel around his waist, beads of water still on the curves of muscle in his chest and shoulders.

He pointed to a bull who was banging his horns against the metal rails on the other side of the pen. "I pick him for Russ. That animal's going to have a bad headache by two o'clock if he keeps that up, and he'll be real irritable."

"Then that's probably the one I'll get," I said.

"I'm going to look at the photography show," he said. "You want to come?"

"No, thanks," I said. "I've got to meet my dad." I had no such plan, but being alone with Kit was making me too tense.

"OK," he said easily. "See you later."

After a moment, even though I told myself I wouldn't, I turned and watched him walk off.

Maybe I *could* go find Dad and the certainty that came from simple conversations about livestock and machinery.

As I cut through the midway, someone grabbed my arm from behind.

It was Russ. "I've got some news for you," he said. He sounded conversational, not his usual belligerent self.

I tried to shrug out of his grasp, but he held on tighter. "What?" I asked.

"It's about your new friend. I thought you'd want to know he's got a reputation at State. As a political activist, you might say."

So Russ had heard, too.

"I'm very happy to hear it," I said. "Now I've got to go."

He tightened his grip. "I'm telling you this for your own good. We may not always see eye to eye, but us guys need to stick together on this."

"Sorry," I said, "I don't know what you mean." But of course I did. And I didn't want to hear what Russ had to say about it. I yanked my arm, but he held fast.

"Hey," he said, "I'm not finished. Don't you know it's rude to leave while somebody's talking?"

"Then why don't you get to the point?"

"Temper, temper," he said. "The point is, your good buddy Kit Crowe is a card-carrying faggot. Not the kind of guy you want to be getting too friendly with."

I jerked my arm away from Russ so hard my hat fell off. "Thanks for sharing," I said. "I'll be seeing you around." My throat was tight from what I wasn't saying as I made myself calmly pick up my hat and walk away.

I leaned against the back of the funnel-cakes booth and took a deep breath. Kit's secret—if it was supposed to be a secret—would be out now. And I couldn't think of anybody worse to be spreading it than Russ—Russ, who thought it was his job to tell you who it was OK for you to be friends with.

Gwen and a couple of her girlfriends came up to the funnel-cakes booth just as I stepped around the corner of it.

"Hi, Johnny," Gwen said, and lowered her eyes.

"Hi, Gwen." I shoved back my hair and plopped my hat on my head. "Hi, Leigh. Hi, Amanda."

"Well, hi yourself," Amanda said.

Leigh twiddled her fingers at me. "Hey."

"You want a funnel cake?" Gwen asked, looking up. "I'll treat." Her cheeks pinked and she looked away from me.

"No, thanks," I said. "I'm about to meet my family for lunch. We'll be eating the two pies my mom decided not to enter in the baking competition as well as the two or three tons of other food she packed for today. I don't want to disappoint her if my capacity's not up to normal. But thanks for the offer. Maybe later, after the rodeo."

"I'll be there to watch you," Gwen said, giving me a quick peek and then looking away again.

What had possessed me to ask her to the dance? She was making us both uncomfortable with her awkward pleasure. If I'd had to ask somebody, why hadn't I asked Amanda? Her reputation might be a little on the questionable side, but at least she knew how to talk to a guy without getting all fluttery. And with Amanda there'd be no expectations. She was always ready to move on to somebody new if things weren't working out. No strings, no broken hearts.

"OK, then," I said. "See you-all later."

"Bye, Johnny," Amanda said. She winked at me. At least I think she did. Or maybe the sun was in her eyes.

Gwen waved, and even Leigh, busy paying for her funnel cake, turned to smile at me. I hated to admit that what Russ had said affected me, but I had to wonder if these girls would be so flirty with me if they knew I was friends with a gay guy.

I went to the picnic grounds even though it was too early. Marty and Paul had just arrived, and I told them I'd play with the baby if they wanted to go look around on their own. Of course, they jumped at the offer.

There's nothing like an hour with a totally demanding creature, who has no idea that you have any concerns other than her, to make you forget about anything else that might be bothering you. By noon, both the baby and I were overjoyed to see her parents show up.

Ten

AFTER LUNCH I WAS BACK AT THE RODEO ARENA. IT was easier to be with the other riders—checking on rigging, stretching, taping, getting psyched—than to stay away and try to pretend I wasn't pulled tight as a fiddle string.

Bobby was there, bouncing up and down on his toes, the black-and-white pattern on his shirt looking like some kind of optical illusion.

"Hey, John," he said. "Where you been? I looked all over and never saw you. But there are plenty of Freddie 4-H'ers and concrete cowboys out there. And the most popular T-shirt this year is the one that says I'VE FALLEN AND I CAN'T GIDDYUP."

"I'll get you one," I said. "How you feeling?"

"Right now I'm wishing I hadn't had ice cream, two hot dogs, three doughnuts, and four rides on the Tilt-a-Whirl."

"I'm wishing I hadn't already had a chat with Russ."

"Yeah, I had one of those, too." He hesitated. "Did he say anything to you about Kit?"

"Yeah."

"You think there's anything to it? Or is Russ just exercising that big mouth of his again?"

I didn't know how to answer. I didn't want to speak for Kit. That information was his to tell, not mine. On the other hand, by his activism at college, he *was* telling it. So I sighed and said, "Yeah. I think it's true. Caroline says he's active in the gay club at State. Does Doug know anything?"

"I don't know. He knew Kit in high school but never said anything about him being…like that. And since Doug didn't go on to State, if it's a new development, he wouldn't know about it." He stopped bouncing on his toes. "Wild," he said. "Kit. I'd never have thought that about him. He looks so…regular. Even better than regular. The kind of guy *I'd* like to be. Except not anymore," he added hastily.

"Does this change anything?" I asked. "Do you like him less than you used to?"

Bobby shook his head. "Boy, I don't know. It creeps me out, you know, wondering if he's going to come on to me or something."

"He could have. At rodeo school. If he'd wanted to."

He laughed. "Hey, watch out or you'll be making me feel bad that he *hasn't* come on to me. What's wrong? I'm not cute enough?" He laughed again and shook his head. "Wild," he said once more. "All of a sudden I feel like that's the only thing I know about him."

"Yeah," I said. "I wonder why we don't think it's just one *more* thing we know about him?"

"Can you imagine him doing it with another guy?" Bobby asked.

It wasn't a picture I really wanted in my head. "Can you imagine your parents doing it?" I asked back.

Bobby made a face. "You're right. There are some things you shouldn't even think about."

"Yeah. And right now you ought to be thinking about running down a calf. You'll be finished long before I ever even get my chance on the bulls."

Kit and Matt came up to us then, carrying their rigging bags, looking like an advertisement for the enduring legend of the cowboy.

"Hey, Bobby, Johnny," Matt said. "You ready to give the fans a show?"

"That's one way of putting it," Bobby said. "Hey, Kit," he added, giving Kit a quick glance and then looking away, reminding me of Gwen's clumsy performance at the funnel-cakes booth.

I wondered if Kit and Matt were more than friends now. Could you tell by looking? At this point I felt like I couldn't tell *anything* by looking.

"Pretty sharp," Kit said to Bobby, admiring his new black-and-white shirt.

Bobby looked startled. I knew exactly what he was thinking. Quickly turning to Matt, he asked, "You think so? You think it's too much?"

Matt laughed. "Are you kidding? You know what peacocks rodeo cowboys are. 'Too much' is a difficult concept for us."

Bobby looked relieved.

Across the dusty expanse behind the chutes, through a crowd of other riders, I could see Russ stretching his legs out against a corral fence. I sent a request into the universe for a bull to stomp on his head with all four feet.

The loudspeaker announced the opening ceremonies. We went to the edge of the arena and crowded up to the fence so we could watch the procession of officials, Miss Westin County Rodeo and her court, various local celebrities, and the color guard, all on their perfectly groomed horses, prance around the ring. The horses were excited and skittish, the same way we were, and they tossed their heads and sidestepped when the procession slowed, then galloped full-out when they got the chance, causing the flags and banners their riders carried to stream dramatically behind them.

The colors, the smells of dust and horseflesh and cotton candy, the march music, and the cheers from the crowd all caused a surge of excitement that made me forget about anything else. I was about to ride on a one-ton bull, a bad-tempered one at that, and all I had to do was hold on for eight seconds. It was a big enough idea to fill my whole head.

I'd drawn the last slot. Everybody else in the entire rodeo would ride before I got my chance. I would be hanging around for hours watching other cowboys blow their own turns—or not. Whatever I did was going to be an anticlimax. In a way, that took a lot of the pressure off. Who would care what I did by the time I went on?

It was an afternoon of major dramas. The bulldoggers got dragged all over the place by steers that just wouldn't go down. One pair of team ropers chased a crafty calf around and around the arena, missing it again and again, while the crowd laughed and shouted advice. Two saddle bronc riders got hung up in their rigging and shaken and stomped pretty bad before the pickup men could get them loose. A bareback rider was thrown and trampled, and left the fairgrounds in an ambulance. And just before my ride, a bull threw his rider and then fell on him, tangling them both in the fencing. Everything stopped while the rider was extracted and put in an ambulance, and the bull was sedated and then removed for examination.

The animal activists who monitor every rodeo made a big deal about that bull, but I knew that rodeo animals are expensive and valuable and very well taken care of. The rough stock can't work more than twice a rodeo, so sixteen seconds is a whole day's work for them. Stock contractors and rodeo officials don't want any trouble, so the animals' welfare comes ahead of the riders'. *Way* ahead.

By the time it was my turn, people were leaving the arena. It was getting late, and there was a lot more fair to see. Besides, a cowboy from a ranch on the other side of the valley had already scored an astonishing eighty-two points on his bull ride, which I knew I couldn't better even on my most golden day; so the show was over, even if the fat lady hadn't sung yet.

I didn't disgrace myself. I stayed on for my eight seconds, mostly because my bull seemed to be thinking that the eight seconds he'd already worked should be an average workday, not sixteen. He gave a lackluster performance, and I was glad when it was over.

My dad came down from the stands, threw one arm around my shoulders and the other around Bobby, and told us we'd done great. He checked out the belt buckle all participants got, which Bobby had already put on his belt.

"Looks good," Dad said. "Next time you'll get the big one."

"I'll sure be trying to," Bobby said.

"That's the spirit," Dad said. He punched me in the shoulder and said, "I suppose you'll be having supper with your date, so we'll see you later at the barn dance."

"Sure, Dad," I said, watching him walk away and disappear in the crowd.

Kit came toward us, limping slightly.

Just before he reached Bobby and me, Russ came at him from the side and clipped him on the shoulder. "Hey there, cupcake," he said. "Had a little trouble out there, didn't you?" Kit had lasted only five seconds on a bull named TNT, who had more than lived up to his name.

Kit clipped Russ's shoulder in return. "Nice of you to be concerned," he said, and turned his back on him, something I wouldn't have done.

"I hope you've got a sweetie waiting to rub your sore places," Russ said.

Kit didn't answer him, just kept walking.

"Hey, I'm talking to you," Russ said.

Kit turned. "I didn't realize that called for an answer."

"Anytime I'm talking to you, it calls for an answer."

"In that case, thank you for your good wishes." Kit kept coming toward Bobby and me. Russ followed him.

"I've been telling your pals what kind of sweetie you're partial to," Russ said. "I guess you hadn't let them know you're an honest-to-God faggot. Or just to be sure they get the message, should I say homo or fairy or fruit or—"

Two rodeo officials who were walking by stopped next to Russ. "Hey, cowboy," one of them said. "Watch that language. You know this fair is a family event, don't you?"

Russ didn't answer. He just kept staring at Kit. One of the officials took him by the arm. "We want to talk to you," he said, and pulled Russ away with him.

Kit took a deep breath and said, "What Russ was saying—"

"It's OK," I said, wanting to stop him, wanting to leave it unsaid. "We know. It's OK." I shouldn't have spoken for Bobby, but I was in a hurry to get past this subject.

"You know?" he said, surprised.

"Caroline," I said. "She sees you on campus."

"Oh. Right," Kit said. "You're OK with it?"

"Sure," I said anxiously. "No problem."

"You're not surprised I'm doing rodeos instead of going to flight-attendant college?" Kit asked, a whisper of bitterness in his voice.

"No, no, not at all," I said.

"Fine with me if you are," Bobby broke in. "Anybody who can give it to Russ the way you do, and sit a bull the way you do is OK, even if you *are* in flight-attendant college."

Kit laughed and reformed the crease in his hat before he put it back on his head.

"Well, I just wanted to say so long before I headed out. I'll be seeing you guys," he said, turning to go.

"Gage County Fair," Bobby called after him. "We get the big belt buckles next time."

Kit turned back to us. "Deal," he said, and kept going.

When he was gone I said to Bobby, "It's really OK with you? About Kit?"

"Well, I kind of had to decide in a hurry, with him right there needing an answer. But yeah, why not? He's an OK guy. What do I care what he does on his own time? As long as he doesn't ask you or me for a date—and why would he—what's it got to do with us? Why are you looking like that? What? You thought my mind was even smaller than it actually is?"

"No, no, I...I don't know what I'm thinking."

"You're saying it's *not* OK with you? You told Kit it was."

"No, I'm not saying that, either. It's just weird is all."

"That's for sure. But I guess we'd better get used to

it. I don't think Kit would be joking about something like that. Hey, I've got to go. Kelsey's waiting for me. We're having dinner before the dance." He gave me one of those looks he always made when he said her name.

"Good," I said. "Have fun. I'll see you later."

It was tempting to think of Bobby as simple, the way he handled things, so out-front and straightforward, with none of the analyzing and agonizing I did that took up so much time and energy, often with so little result. Now, for the first time, it occurred to me that he was more clear-sighted than I was, which made it easier for him to make decisions and live with them. Kit was gay; Bobby wasn't. Those were the facts; end of story.

Easy for Bobby. Not so easy for me.

God. I'd forgotten all about Gwen. A whole evening ahead with her, when all I wanted was a long hot shower and a long cool nap, with my head empty and Howdy lying on my feet.

And there she came, out of the stands.

"Hi," she said. "Are you OK? You look funny."

"I'm fine. You want to go get some dinner?"

We ate. We danced. I even danced with Kelsey while Bobby danced with Gwen. Kelsey and I were careful and polite with each other, and both of us, I think, were glad when our dance was finished. Gwen and I were equally careful and polite. It definitely wasn't her fault we couldn't get going, but I could tell she thought it was and it made her feel bad. Which made me feel bad. But it's there or it's not, and with us, it wasn't.

At nine-thirty we went outside and sat on hay bales to watch the fireworks. I could see Kelsey's head on Bobby's shoulder, while Gwen and I sat stiffly beside each other, dutifully saying, "Oooh," and, "Aaah."

When it was time to say good night, I gave Gwen a quick hug and a little kiss, and I think we both understood we'd never be going out again.

I felt like a worm.

Eleven

FOR THE NEXT TWO WEEKS, I PUT MY HEAD DOWN AND worked. I mended fences. I moved cattle to new pasture. I made house and barn repairs. I taught Windy the foal how to load into a horse trailer, learning again that the most important thing you need when training a horse is more time than the horse. I sweat gallons and got a tan that stopped halfway up my biceps and in the middle of my forehead.

Dad was more than pleased at how much help I was giving him, letting him get some of his neglected paperwork done. Clemmie was not, since I was always too busy to play with her or to go for rides—though my stomach was always available for sitting on to watch TV, since by evening, I was completely totaled. I was too occupied and too wiped out to do much thinking—and I didn't miss it.

When Bobby called, suggesting another trip to Kit's to practice on the mechanical bull, I told him I couldn't go, I was too tied up, which wasn't true. He went without me and reported that they'd had a fine day, very laid-back. Matt had been there, too, and a couple of other guys, neither of whom seemed like fairies except one, maybe, whose jeans were ironed into creases. And yeah, Kit was the same as ever, and it was still really hard to believe he was what he said he was.

I wished then that I'd gone, that I hadn't been so cowardly or apprehensive or just plain stupid or whatever it was that had kept me at home. But I wouldn't let my mind stay on that subject for very long. It bounced and skittered away, still cowardly and apprehensive.

We packed for the Gage County Fair as if it were an expedition to Antarctica: Sally's collection, Mom's pecan pies, piles of food and changes of clothes, and people. We needed the van *and* the pickup to haul everything. Then there were the last-minute trips back to the house for forgotten items and a final bathroom stop for Clemmie—wearing her GREATEST SHOW ON DIRT T-shirt—who would be riding with me in the truck.

"I tried not to be," she said, as we caravanned out of the yard behind Dad's van, "but I'm mad at you."

"Ah, don't be mad, Clemmie. It'll give you wrinkles."

"I can't help that. I'm mad anyway. So is Howdy."

"Howdy, too? What have I done to you both?"

"You haven't played with us. You work too much."

"Well, I have to help Dad. You and Howdy can play with each other. You don't need me."

"Yes, we do. We do need you. It's not as fun without you. Howdy can't make jokes."

I hadn't been feeling very jokey the past couple of weeks. I was pretty sure Howdy would be better company than me any day. And better at jokes, too. I knew he had a good sense of humor.

"OK, OK. Tell you what, Clemmie. You can have me all day today, except for the time I have to ride in the rodeo. We'll do whatever you want."

"Anything? Really? You'll go pet the lambs and ride on the Tilt-a-Whirl, and make paper airplanes at the craft place?"

I sighed. Penance.

"Anything you want," I said.

So we petted the lambs and rode on the rides and spent an eternity at the craft place, making unrecognizable things from construction paper and paper clips and lots of glue. We ran into Bobby once on the midway, where I was buying Clemmie a pile of Australian battered fries she'd insisted on and I knew she'd never finish.

"Hey, John," he said. "You want to go do something?"

Clemmie grabbed my hand and held on tight, but she didn't say anything.

"Can't, man," I said. "My date here is very possessive."

"Got rug-rat duty? My sympathies." He took one of Clemmie's fries as she squawked, "Hey!" and put them behind her back. "You're still riding today, right?"

"Absolutely. That's the only time off I get."

"You going to the barn dance?"

"With me, right?" Clemmie said. "Who are you going with, Bobby?"

Bobby gave me that guilty look, and I knew he'd be with Kelsey.

"It's OK," I said. "She and I are finished. Remember?"

"Yeah. I know. It's just weird. I really like her."

"Well, great. Go for it."

"Yeah?" he mumbled. "You're not taking Gwen?"

"He's going with *me,*" Clemmie repeated.

"That's right," I said. "Clemmie's my main squeeze today. Gwen and I, well, it wasn't written in the stars."

"Boy, you must have got caught doing something major to have to work all the time *and* do the baby-sitting," Bobby said. "You can fill me in before the rodeo."

"I'll see you later," I said as Clemmie dragged me away down the midway.

I actually had fun with her—she was a funny little kid—but half a day was long enough. After the whole-family lunch at the picnic grounds, I went, with relief, off to the rodeo arena.

"Don't get stomped!" she yelled after me. "We're dancing tonight, remember?"

"I can't decide which sounds more like punishment!" I hollered back.

Only when I was making my way across the fair-grounds did I realize I'd been looking through the crowds all morning—as I was doing still—for a glimpse of Kit.

I saw him before he saw me. Even from the back I knew it was him—one leg braced on a fence rail, stretching it out. I stopped and just looked at him. He wasn't doing anything different from any of the other cowboys preparing to ride, but he held my attention in a way none of the rest of them did. His grace, his fine proportions, his self-possession.

While I stood there, Matt came up beside me. "Hey, John. Ready to ride?"

I looked at him and blinked, like I was waking myself up. "Hey, Matt. Sure. Always ready. How about you?"

"Always ready to get my physique rearranged. We missed you last week at Kit's."

"Yeah, well, my dad's been busy, and he couldn't spare me. Bobby said it was a good day."

"Riding and eating—how could it not be," Matt said. "Ah, there's Kit." He pointed and started in that direction. I went along, wondering as I did what, if anything, was going on between Matt and Kit.

Kit looked up and saw us coming. He raised his hand in greeting. "Matt. John. Ready for some punishment?"

"Bring it on," Matt said.

"Too dumb to know better," I said. I saw nothing special in Kit's greeting to Matt. Did that make me feel better?

"Too bad you missed practicing on the bull Saturday," Kit said.

"Couldn't be helped," I said.

Kit gave me a long look. "Sure," he said.

Bobby joined us then, and we all did the things, necessary and superstitious, we had to do to get ready to ride.

When Matt and Bobby went off to the chutes for the calf roping, Kit came and leaned on the fence beside me where I was halfheartedly stretching and feeling like the underside of a snake.

"You OK?" he asked.

"I look like I'm not?" It came out more smart-mouthed than I intended—only because I didn't know what to say. Was Kit just concerned, the way you would be with any friend? Or was it something more? I didn't know how to tell.

"Sorry," Kit said, backing away. "I didn't mean to intrude."

"No," I said, turning around. "*I'm* sorry. I didn't mean that the way it sounded. I just meant, well, why would you ask? Do I seem like I'm not OK?"

"You seem distracted. Distant. Like something's on your mind. Something besides getting on a bull's back, I mean. And I'm wondering if it has anything to do with what you know about me."

I couldn't think fast enough to straighten out all the thoughts that came pouring into my mind—about him, about myself—questions I needed answered, explanations I needed to make.

"I thought so," he said. He stepped back from the railing. "You know," he said quietly, "I'm tired of explaining myself. I thought with you maybe I wouldn't have to."

Just as he was turning to go, I said, "Wait a minute. It's not what you think. I'm...my mind is so full I can't think, that's all. Don't go. You don't have to explain anything. But can you just tell me why you thought you wouldn't have to with me?"

"Because I thought you would understand what it's like to be different."

"Why?" I asked, standing very still.

"You told me," he said. "One of those nights out at the corral. Don't you remember? Your heart surgery. You told me that made you feel different."

"Oh. Well, yeah. But not the way you do. I mean, it's not the same thing, is it? I mean, how can you compare?..." What was I doing? He was telling me he wanted to be friends—what was *I* telling *him*? Why couldn't I just say that I was still shell-shocked about his being gay, that I didn't know what that meant as far as he and I were concerned, that his difference made him strange to me but, at the same time, I liked him as much as I ever had and I didn't know how to be with him now.

I wished I didn't know. Then we could just be the way we were before, easy and good together.

"I see," he said quietly. "OK. But just so you know, I do get the difference between friendship and romance. You wouldn't have to be afraid of me." He walked away, toward the chutes.

"That's not it," I called after him. But he kept going.

And as he did, I realized that that *was* it. I was protecting myself from having to decide what to do when he hit on me—something I assumed was inevitable. And something that I dreaded and, oddly, awaited curiously.

I stood at the fence rail, replaying what I'd said, fixing it, making it turn out differently, until I heard the announcer say that bull riding would be the next event. I was up second, so I hustled over to the chutes, as unprepared as I could possibly be.

I rode like I had lead in my head and none in my seat. My neck jerked around so much it hurt for days afterward, and following the bull's first jump, my butt never touched his back again. I was in the air before I knew what was happening, and hit the ground so hard I wondered if my teeth had shattered. What was I, nuts? Doing this when I could be with Clemmie, eating cotton candy and admiring somebody's prize-winning rabbits? Instead I was lousing up the most interesting friendship I'd ever had and damn near getting my neck broken by a deranged candidate for Burger King.

As I dragged myself out of the arena, I could see Kit on a bull's back in the chutes. I was definitely not a hard act to follow.

I leaned on the fence and watched him, a perfect illustration of *right* contrasted with my illustration of *wrong.* He stayed on for eight seconds, plus a little. He looked great, steady and graceful and strong. His bull was a mean one, too, which meant more points. I knew he would win.

He did. I hung around, while trying to look as if I wasn't, waiting for him to collect his check and his belt buckle, waiting for another chance to explain myself if he would let me.

My dad came looking for me, Clemmie in tow.

"Let's wait for your pal Kit. I've been wanting to meet him ever since you told me about him from rodeo school. I won't get a better chance than this. He looked terrific, like he'd been riding bulls all his life. A natural."

Hadn't Mom told Dad about Kit? She hadn't said anything about my going over to Kit's to ride on the bull, so maybe she'd decided to keep it to herself until there was a reason to tell.

Or maybe it was a subject she didn't find decent enough for discussion. Who ever knew with her?

"Can't we go?" Clemmie asked. "I want to throw the darts at the balloons again. I want to win the panda bear. Johnny has to come with me."

"I don't know how long Kit will be," I said, losing my nerve. "I could go with Clemmie and you could meet him another time."

"It won't hurt to hang around a couple more minutes," Dad said. "Clemmie can be patient, can't you, cowgirl?" Clemmie nodded, but she wasn't happy about it.

Just then Kit came out of the office trailer. He hesitated when he saw me.

"Isn't that him?" Dad asked.

He stepped toward Kit, his hand out. "I just want to congratulate you. John told me about you after rodeo school, and I can see he wasn't exaggerating. You looked good out there." It was pretty clear to me that Dad was clueless about Kit. Something in his attitude would have shown if he'd known, I was sure of it.

"Thanks," Kit said.

"Can I see the buckle?" Clemmie asked. "They keep talking about it."

Kit grinned at her, a natural, pleasant grin that made him look like a movie star. He handed her the buckle. "You can win one of your own someday," he said. "You know that? I can tell good riders from those who couldn't ride in a boxcar with both doors shut, and I'll bet you're a good rider already."

"I am," she said, holding the big buckle in both hands.

"Then, think about it. Having your own buckle is better than looking at somebody else's."

I could see the idea take root in Clemmie's head. In two seconds, just with the force of his personality, Kit had inspired her. I was as impressed as she was.

"I need to go now," Kit said, "but you know what? I'm not going to forget that your fingerprints are on my buckle, and I'm going to be waiting for a day when I can put mine on *your* buckle."

"OK," she said solemnly, handing him back the buckle as if it were the Holy Grail. "You won't forget?"

"I never forget," he said.

"I can remind him if he does," I blurted.

Kit just looked at me.

"Kit and I are friends, you know, Clemmie," I went on. "I'll make sure he doesn't forget."

Kit was quiet for a minute, thinking, and then he said, "So, John. You want to come over tomorrow and practice on the bull?"

"I'd say he needs it," my dad put in. "Wouldn't you?"

"John's a good rider," Kit said. "Anybody can have one bad ride. Eight seconds isn't much of a chance to show what you can do."

"All the more impressive when you do it, then," Dad said. "That was quite a ride *you* made."

"Thanks." Then he looked at me again, waiting for an answer.

Dad had made it plain he had no objections to my taking the next day off, so my excuse, if I'd wanted one, was gone. "OK. Sure. What time?"

"Whenever you get there," Kit said. "Nice to meet you, sir," he said, shaking hands with my father. Then he shook Clemmie's hand, too. "Get to work," he told her. "You can be a star."

"OK," she said. "I will."

As Kit walked off, Dad said, "Nice boy. One of those lucky ones; born with everything."

TWELVE

ON SUNDAY DAD WOULDN'T LET ME LOITER AROUND the house. "Aren't you ready to go yet?" he asked. "I don't need you. Why don't you get on over to Kit's? The bull's a-waiting. Monroe County Fair's in two weeks. You want your eight seconds to count then, don't you?"

"You sound like you're trying to get rid of me."

"That's right," he said. "Beat it."

When I drove into Kit's yard, he came out of the house, the screen door banging behind him. He walked over to the pickup, his hands in his back pockets. "I wondered if you'd come," he said.

"I said I would." Still, I sat in the truck.

Neither of us spoke. Then Kit said, "Do you want to get out of the truck?"

After a few seconds I opened the door and jumped down.

"I've got to pick some blackberries for my mom," he

said. "You can come with me." He went back to the porch and returned with two metal pails. He handed one to me and headed around the side of the house, across the barnyard, onto a path that led to a little creek with a tangle of berry bushes growing along it. I followed mutely. We came to a place where the bushes were so thick we could no longer see the house. Kit pulled berries off the vines, dropping them into his bucket. He didn't say anything, so I knew it was up to me to start. But I didn't know how.

"I don't know what to say," I said.

"Maybe by telling me why I scare you."

"You don't…," I began, but then knew I was lying. And that was no way to have the friendship I wanted with him. He waited. "OK. Maybe *scare* is too strong a word. But *nervous*. That's more how I feel."

He stayed quiet, waiting some more.

"I can't imagine your life," I said.

"You thought you could. Before you knew. You thought it was pretty much the same as yours."

"Except for—" I didn't know what words to use.

"Except for *who*," he said. "Everything else is similar. I like a lot of the same things you do—we talked about those at rodeo school when we couldn't sleep. I want work I love. I want, eventually, to find a partner for my life. I want to have friends and good times. Why does that make you nervous? Never mind. I know.

"Let me tell you something. I've already found out that the absolutely last thing I ever want to do is come on to a straight guy, so that won't be a problem if I can help it. Do you think I should have to hang out just with other gay guys?"

"Well, no—," I began.

"It's tempting," he interrupted me. "It's easier. But I don't want my life to be that narrow. I also don't want to hide who I am, though I don't broadcast it, either. You don't have to go around declaring you're straight, so why should I always have to announce I'm gay?"

"When did you know?" Finally I was able to ask a question.

"I've known since I was seven."

"Seven!"

"Well, I knew something was different about me that early, and when puberty—or hormonal insanity, as I think of it—set in, it just got clearer. Not everybody figures it out that soon, though."

"What about telling people? Your family? How did you do that?"

"I kept quiet about myself until I went to college. It was just easier. In some ways. Harder in others, because it was lonely. And dishonest. But now my parents know. And my sister, too. She's cool with it. Just since Christmas, though. Being away at school made it easier to get up my nerve to tell them. And no, my parents aren't thrilled. First they didn't believe I was sure, and then they wanted me to get counseling, which my sister told them was a waste of time. Now they just don't mention it. They'll probably get used to it someday, but they're also probably never going to like it. I just knew I couldn't keep hiding such a central part of myself. It made me feel wrong, and that made me feel ashamed. I didn't want to feel like that anymore."

"What about people who won't like you because of what you are?"

"That can be pretty harsh," he said. "Some of them hate me, some would like to hurt me, and some might even want to kill me. My sister has some theory about how guys who hate gays are really uncertain about their own orientation, but I say that's BS. They're just haters, and gay isn't the only thing they hate. A few of them have said some ugly things to me, that's for sure. And I have to bear it. What's the choice? I can't keep hiding." He pulled a couple of blackberries off a bush and stuck them in his mouth. "I don't know why this is so hard for other people. It has nothing to do with them; just with me."

"Yeah. I don't know, either." I studied the few berries in the bottom of my pail. My brain was still boiling with thoughts, but Kit was seeming like Kit again, and not some fearful stranger. How could I have forgotten what he was like?

"Come on," Kit said. "Why don't we finish with these berries and get over to the bull." He started pulling berries off the bushes. "I hope you know there's more to a person than just a libido."

I'd have to look that word up when I got home. (I did. It means "the instinctual sexual impulse.")

I stayed a couple of hours. I picked the berries and practiced on the bull and had some lunch. Kit poured iced tea and opened cans of chili. He said that was the extent of his cooking skills and I shouldn't have any delusions about his gourmet capacities just because of his orientation.

All the way home my brain kept boiling. But now it was boiling about me, not about Kit. How big a jerk was I, is what I wanted to know. I still liked Kit. He was cool and strong and interesting, and I wanted his friendship. But I wondered what people would think about me if we were friends. Would they assume I was gay, too? Would they assume Kit and I were getting it on? Was gayness catching? Did the fact that I could remember exactly what Kit looked like when he got out of the shower mean I'd already caught it? What about the fact that I thought about him more than I'd ever thought about Bobby, my best friend? Or Kelsey, for that matter?

By the time I got home I had such a headache that, even though I knew Mom would lose it if she found out, I smuggled Howdy upstairs to take a nap with me. I just wanted to get away from my busy mind for a while and have his doggy devotion and furry comfort.

We got away with it, but the nap didn't quiet my mind for long.

I kept going through my daily routines of chores and helping Dad and coaching Clemmie—up on Peaches every day, turning herself into the champion Kit knew she could be—and I stewed.

I didn't even want to go to the Monroe Fair, where

I'd see Kit again in public. Why couldn't we just be friends in private?

How could it be that no one knew what was happening inside me? I wasn't such a good actor; it was simply that everyone accepted me as part of the everyday landscape. They thought they knew me.

Eventually, oddly, Mom noticed. Something. She didn't know what, but she knew something was bugging me.

"You OK, Johnny?" she asked. She never called me Johnny anymore. Hadn't since I was ten or eleven.

"Sure," I lied. "Why?"

"I don't know. You seem—I don't know." She even brushed back my hair and put her hand on my forehead, feeling for fever.

"How about a piece of pie?" she asked.

"Pecan?" I'd had all of that that I wanted for a long time to come.

She laughed. "No. I'm sick of it, too. Lemon."

"Yeah. That'd be good."

Her solicitude bothered me as much as the indifference I was more used to. What had she noticed? Did she think I was afraid of riding again, at the Monroe Fair, after being bounced off the bull? Was she watching to see if any of Kit's "indecency" was rubbing off on me? Or did she see something else? Something that even I wasn't aware of?

THIRTEEN

THE DAY BEFORE THE MONROE COUNTY FAIR, THUNderheads built up behind the mountains on the horizon, dark piles of clouds with lightning flashes inside them. The grumble of thunder was in the background all afternoon, and the light was gray and heavy. Just before dinner it started to rain—at first a gentle patter, and then, into the night, a steadier downpour.

It was still raining in the morning.

"Doesn't look like a great day for a county fair," Dad said, leaning against the kitchen counter, a cup of coffee in his hand.

"We're still going, right, Daddy? Clemmie asked anxiously. "I want to tell Kit I've been practicing."

"I don't know, baby," Dad said. "The midway won't be much fun in the rain."

"Yes, it will," Clemmie said. "I'll wear my raincoat. And my boots, too."

"Sweetie, it'll be very muddy," Mom said.

"I don't *care,*" she said, her lower lip coming out. She dropped her spoon into her cereal. "You have to take your pies. You won last time and you want another ribbon, I know you do." She was bringing out the big guns now. Working on Mom's vanity.

"My pies'll be in the state fair, anyway. I don't need this one."

"But Sally's collection. She still needs to win a ribbon so she can take it to the state fair."

Sally came through the kitchen door then. "What about my collection?"

"Daddy's thinking about not going to the fair," Clemmie said.

"But, Dad," Sally exclaimed, "we *have* to go. My collection has to win today or it won't go to the state fair. I'll have a better chance when it's raining. Some people will stay home. The competition will be less." She looked at me. "For Johnny, too. In the rodeo."

I'd just been thinking the weather was a perfect excuse for not going to the fair. The rodeo wouldn't be canceled; rodeos were never called on account of weather. But I could cancel myself.

"What about this," Dad said. "How about if the ladies and I go for the pie and collection judging and then come home. John can take the pickup and come home after the rodeo. That way Mom's and Sally's things can be entered in the competitions, Clemmie and I can do a turn around the midway, and we can get home before we drown. How's that sound?"

"So it's OK if *I* drown?" I asked. "I was thinking I might skip this one."

"Don't tell me you're afraid of a little mud," he said. "You're no pansy, John. You've paid your entry fee. Now you have to cowboy up."

Arguing with Dad was pointless. And the last thing I wanted to be was a pansy. I knew I'd have to go, even though the arena would be hip-deep in mud.

"Falls hurt less in mud," Dad said. "It's softer than dirt."

"You're right," I said, giving up. I could still hope that the weather would keep Kit home, though I knew that wasn't the way he operated.

Dad put his hand on my shoulder. "That's my boy. Nothing stops him. And I guarantee you, all the real cowboys will be there," he said. "Then that's how we'll do it, if it's OK with the rest of you."

"Maybe it'll stop raining and then we can stay longer," Clemmie said.

"Maybe," Dad conceded, "but the forecast says different."

"What *does* it say?" Mom asked.

"It's supposed to get worse," Dad said. "Couple more days of rain."

"Oh, Cy," Mom said, "do you really think it's all right to go?"

"I think it'll be OK. We'll be home before dark."

I was surprised, when we got to the fairgrounds, to see how many other people had driven through the rain and parked in the mud just as we had.

The downpour was a relief from the terrific heat we'd been having, and there was a sense of celebration in being out in it. The temperature was warm enough that we didn't mind getting wet, and there was the clean smell of ozone and grateful vegetation in the air. Damp people under umbrellas rushed to the indoor exhibits. Hardier folks took the midway rides, huddling gamely together at the top of the Ferris wheel, whooping bravely on the Twister. I thought I'd be able to identify Kit, even if I couldn't see anything but his umbrella, which he wouldn't really be carrying—real cowboys didn't use them—because I'd been thinking about him so much. But if he was on the midway, I didn't spot him.

I did run into Bobby—the brim of his hat, like mine, shedding cascades onto his shoulders—carrying a bag with his rodeo clothes in it. "I don't know why I'm going to bother to change," he said. "I'll be soaked in a second. But I think it's important, you know?"

"Yeah, I know. Look your best and you do your best."

"That's it. In any situation. See, the way I figure it is, if you start cutting corners because things aren't just perfect, you lose your edge when they are. One hundred percent, all the time."

"You're fired up," I said.

"Got to be to make myself go out in the mud, knowing what's going to happen to my hot new shirt. I bought four new ones, you know. One for each fair. And I'm not going to wear an old shirt today, no matter what. My new shirt'll keep me psyched."

"Well, go for it," I said. "I wish I had some kind of magic charm."

"I've been thinking; wondering if getting superstitious is such a good idea. If something goes wrong with your charm, like, if I tear my shirt before my ride or spill ketchup on it, will I take that as a bad omen and get all freaked?"

"I don't know, Bobby. But it's always good to have something to blame a less-than-stellar performance on. If you ride bad, it's because your shirt tore. Couldn't be helped."

"You got a point there, Gentleman John. You going over to the arena?"

"Sure." I wished I could worry about the kind of things Bobby worried about. It would be so much more restful than what was going on in my mind.

A tent had been rigged behind the rodeo arena, where the cowboys could stretch, wait, and prepare for their rides. Inside, it was steamy and full of the smells of animals and overheated humanity. I knew some rodeos were held in indoor arenas, but to me, rodeos would always mean outdoor summer skies—rain or shine—and the fresh outdoor smells. Even manure smells better outside than in.

The sound of the rain on the canvas tent top was loud and distracting, and I could tell it was not just me who was having trouble getting into the right mental state to take on several hundred pounds of dumb animal.

"Hi, John. Bobby." Kit arrived suddenly, his hair wet and slicked back, his hat in his hand. After all the time

I'd spent looking for him, when he did show up, he caught me by surprise.

"Hey, Kit," Bobby said, giving him a high five. "Nice day, huh?"

"Beautiful. It's going to be a lot of fun out there. Matt won't be here," Kit went on. "He broke his ankle falling down the stairs at home. Pretty poor excuse, if you ask me. I think he's just too chicken about getting dirty."

"That sounds like Matt," I said.

I'd expected at least a smile, but I didn't get one. When Kit looked at me, his gray eyes were level and calm.

"Doesn't it?" he said. "Have you checked the lineup? Do you know when we ride?"

"I was just going to go do that," I said.

"I'll go with you," he said. Turning to Bobby, he asked, "You want us to check out your time?"

"Sure," Bobby said, squatting, rummaging in his rigging bag. "No tricks, though, OK? Don't tell me they've left me off the list. Or put me in with the bull riders."

"Would we do that to our pal Bob?" Kit asked. "No way."

He and I headed across the big tent, jigging around clots of cowboys toward the flap that led into the office trailer where the buckles, trophies, and prize money were kept. We didn't speak. Posted on the wall inside was the list of who rode, in what order, on which animal.

"I see you have your old friend Mixmaster," Kit said.

"I might as well go home right now and deprive everybody of a laugh."

"You ride after me this time," he said.

"No need for me to ride at all, then."

"And Russ rides after you."

"Well, there's a reason to hang around. He's got to come off that bull, whether he lasts two seconds or ten. He ought to make a pretty big splash."

He put his finger on Bobby's name. "Look here."

"They've got him down as a steer wrestler," I said. "Poor Bobby."

"You think he'll believe us when we tell him?"

"You tell him. He'll believe you."

Kit just looked at me, one eyebrow raised, then turned back toward the tent.

We watched the cowboys go one by one out of the tent into the rain, then come back cursing and muddy. The animals slid and staggered in the arena, kicking up clots of mud that splattered everywhere. The covered stands were full—with people who were probably feeling saner than usual because they, at least, knew enough to stay out of the rain while we were not only out in it but were out in it on big, irritated animals.

Contrary to what you might think, there weren't a lot of injuries. Even when animals fell, the wet earth had some give to it or cowboy and animal slid away from each other, so that getting filthy was a bigger problem than getting broken.

Kit's ride on the appropriately named Stormy Weather was flawless. Both he and the bull were in top form. Kit's navy blue shirt with white piping didn't even look wet; it just looked shiny. He was as graceful as ever, as controlled, as calm. That day, it was impossible to do better than he did.

I had my best ride since rodeo school, but even though Mixmaster was a fine rank bull—only slightly less homicidal than he'd been at rodeo school—and I stayed on for all eight seconds, I knew my score wouldn't be as high as Kit's. As usual he had looked like the text-book demonstration for how it should be done.

Russ rode after me. I could see how much he wanted to win, just by the set of his shoulders and head. And that was his mistake. He was too stiff, too desperate; he tried too hard. And he landed in the mud, face first, in about four seconds.

He stormed into the tent, wet and muddy and under a full head of steam, came straight to Kit, and shoved him hard with both hands, in the center of Kit's chest.

Kit took a couple of steps backward. "Hey!" he said. "What's your problem?"

Curious faces from all through the tent turned in their direction.

"I can't believe I got beat by a fag, that's my problem," Russ said. "Why don't you quit, you fairy, and leave bull riding to real men?" He came after Kit and shoved him again.

Kit's eyes narrowed. If he was worried about having his private business broadcast through the tent, he didn't show it. "You think the bulls can tell the difference?" he asked. His hands were still at his sides, not even raised in self-defense.

Russ wasn't going to let him stay that way. He wanted

a fight. "Aren't you even gonna take a poke at me, Queenie? You gonna just let me push you around? But why not? You haven't got any balls, have you?"

I literally saw red. My vision was so blinded by rage, I probably couldn't have located Russ to wallop him. But this had nothing to do with me, I warned myself. This was Kit's business.

"Hey, hold it, Russ," Bobby said, running interference. "Don't be such a sore loser."

But Russ wouldn't be distracted. It was Kit he was after.

"I'm not getting disqualified for fighting," Kit said, "if that's what you're trying to do. But even if I did, you'd still be a loser."

"Your sweetheart's right behind you," Russ said. "You get DQ'ed and sweet Johnny gets the prize. Nice, the way you queers stick together."

At that my red rage erupted like a burst pipe. I grabbed Russ by the back of his shirt collar and swung him around to face me. Without even thinking or aiming, I hit him square in the face with my clenched fist. The blow hurt my hand, and as I shook it out, I wondered what I was trying to prove. Hitting Russ had until now been something I avoided as much as I could. It had never been known to change his mind about anything, anyway.

Russ's nose started to bleed instantly, a red bloom in the middle of his face. At that the other cowboys crowded in on us, pulling us apart.

Officials came then and wasted no time in disqualifying me for fighting. Kit had won that day in more than bull riding. He'd stayed cool and smart, and hadn't let Russ stampede him the way I had, though he had more reason.

"All cowboys clear the tent," the loudspeaker boomed, just as we were getting our mess straightened out. "Because of nearby lightning strikes, this area is being cleared. Please go immediately to a safer location."

"Come on," Kit said to me and Bobby. "I've got my dad's motor home. We'll be safe in there."

FOURTEEN

WE RAN THROUGH THE RAIN TO THE MOTOR HOME. It was noisy inside with the rain pounding on the metal skin and the thunder crashing nearby.

"Wild!" Bobby shouted over the noise. "What a day!" He sat in the driver's seat, his hands on the wheel. "Nice vehicle."

"My mom made me drive it today. Because of the weather. Want a drink?" he asked, opening the little refrigerator. "Coke, root beer, or Gatorade?"

We got our drinks and sat—Bobby still in the driver's seat, me in the passenger's, and Kit on the bench at the table—watching the rain. We might as well have been underwater for all that we could see through the window.

"Russ is an idiot," Bobby finally said.

"News flash," Kit said.

"True," Bobby said, nodding.

"I've got to get used to people like him," Kit said.

126

"Of course, I don't like it, but what am I going to do? Beat them all up? Even if I'd like to, I don't think that'd work."

"It's not an easy thing to get used to," Bobby said.

"No, you're right," Kit agreed. "Not yet, anyway."

Bobby drained his drink and stood up. "I've got to meet up with my parental units. Want a ride, John?"

"Thanks. I've got the pickup." Maybe he was waiting for me to say I had to go, too. But I didn't say that. I sat where I was. I understood that I was making some kind of a decision, but I didn't know what it was.

"Well, OK, then," Bobby said. "See you." He went out into the deluge.

Kit and I sat in silence, looking at each other, listening to the rain.

"Why did you hit Russ?" Kit asked. "I thought you avoided fighting."

"Russ needed hitting," I said.

"I can take care of myself, you know," he said.

"He brought me into it, too."

"Oh, I see. You were proving something."

"Anything wrong with that?"

"Not as long as you know who you're proving it to."

Who *had* I been proving it to? Kit? I didn't think so. Russ? Was hitting him going to convince him I wasn't gay if that's what he'd decided? Nope.

Myself?

Why?

"Do you?" Kit asked.

"Maybe," I said.

I sat there watching him for his reaction, waiting for it. But he said nothing. His hair was wet, falling across his forehead, and while I hated to admit it, he just looked beautiful to me. I wanted to sit there talking to him, and at the same time, I was wishing I'd never met him.

Rain hammered on the metal roof, the sound of an endless clatter of hooves.

I cleared my throat and spoke. "Do you have a..." I didn't know what the right word was.

"No," he said. "Not now." Then he just looked at me.

I couldn't think of the next thing to say.

Kit sighed. "I thought we were past this. Are you thinking I'm some kind of freak show?" he asked. "Because if you are, you can leave now."

"No," I said quickly. "That's not it."

"Well, then, what is it? You make me nervous, the way you watch me all the time. You don't do that with anybody else."

When I didn't say anything, he said, "I'm not a specimen for you to examine like some scientist. I'm trying to figure out my life the same way you are. I don't have answers."

"I know." But I wasn't sure I meant it. I thought he must have some answers.

I got up and wandered around, looking at the way everything was so compact and shipshape in the motor home. Standing behind Kit where he couldn't see me, I said, "I don't always know why I do things."

"Me, either," Kit said. "But there *is* a reason, even if

it takes awhile to figure out what it is. You have to trust your instincts."

"I can't always do that, either," I said, feeling my sore hand.

"Yeah. I know. Understanding yourself is a bitch, isn't it? How are we supposed to ever understand anybody else?"

"Sometimes that seems easier."

He made a skeptical sound.

"Well, how do you explain friendship, then?" I asked.

"One of those times you have to trust your instincts," he said. "Something just clicks."

I wanted to ask him if he'd heard that click at rodeo school with me. I'd heard it with him. But I couldn't ask.

I sat down across from him again. "So, how about them Rockies?"

Kit laughed. "How about them?"

"What's your favorite sport? What's your favorite team? What's your favorite statistic?"

He told me. And we kept talking; first about sports and then about music and then about working on ranches, which got us to talking about our families. Somewhere in there Kit made cocoa and we kept talking.

"I'm starving," Kit said.

I looked at my watch. It was almost ten o'clock. "No wonder. We've been sitting here for five hours."

"There's food here. We can fix something. Then I have to go. We're supposed to be out of the parking lot by eleven."

"I should go call home. My mom'll think I'm off somewhere looking for trouble. Wait'll she finds out I was DQ'ed for fighting."

Kit let me use the phone in the motor home.

"Take it easy on the way home," my dad said. "It's still raining pretty hard. How'd you do?"

"Good. Made my time but lost on points." I'd explain about being disqualified if and when I had to, but I hoped this incident wouldn't ever get to Dad.

"Can't win them all," Dad said. "But I'll bet you're glad you showed up. See you later."

We made sandwiches and kept talking while we ate. We'd gotten past some kind of barrier, and we had as much to talk about as we'd had those nights on the corral fence at rodeo school.

Just before eleven I rose to leave. With the door open and the rain coming down hard behind me, I turned back to Kit. "Can I still come over to use the bull?"

"Why not?" he asked.

"Will you come over to see Clemmie? She wants to show you how well she rides."

"Sure. Just say when."

"OK. See you."

I ran through the rain to the pickup. As I was unlocking the door, a truck across the parking lot started up. Its lights came on and it headed toward me, fast, splashing mud from its wheels. It stopped next to me just as I got the door to the truck opened.

The window came down and Russ leaned out. "Hey, bunny butt," he said, "have a good time?"

"Beating you on points?" I asked, climbing into the truck's cab. "Yeah. I really liked that." The rain fell hard between our trucks. I started to pull my door closed.

"That's not what I mean," he said. "I mean did you have a good time snuggling with your sweetie in there?" He hooked his thumb toward the motor home, which was just pulling out of the lot. "I see Bobby left you and the kitten alone. So thoughtful of him to let you have your little fun together."

He'd seen Bobby leave? Had he been sitting there all this time watching us?

"You don't know anything," I said.

"All I can say is, this is going to come as a big relief to Kelsey. She won't have to wonder anymore what she did wrong. Her only problem is she's a girl, which I see is not your gender of preference."

My anger flared. "You don't know what you're talking about. And leave Kelsey out of this." Even though I knew it would accomplish nothing, even though I knew it was completely contrary to what I thought about myself, I'd have hit him again if I could have reached him.

"OK," he said genially. His shirtsleeve on the windowsill was getting soaked, but he was in no hurry to go. "I've got a good enough story without her."

Talk was useless. So I called Russ a name—one I'd never said out loud before—and gunned the pickup out of there, throwing a fan of mud against the side of his truck as I went. But I could hear him laughing as I drove away.

FIFTEEN

WHEN I PULLED INTO THE YARD, HOWDY CAME RUN-
ning, his curly white fur muddy and sodden,
shining in the reflection from the security lights. He always waited for me to come home, no matter how late it
was or how bad the weather. He wouldn't go to sleep
until I was there. His tongue was out; he was grinning,
deliriously happy to see me.

He jumped up on me when I got out of the truck,
but I was already so muddy from the rodeo it didn't matter. I hugged him hard and took him inside with me. I
dried him with a towel and put him out on the utility
porch to sleep, before I went up to bed. It was a long
time till I was able to close my eyes.

I was dead out of it when Clemmie jumped on my
bed in the morning.

"The lights went out last night, and we had to have
candles at dinner," she announced.

"Yeah?" I mumbled, groggy and disoriented.

"Did you see Kit? I never saw him. Did you tell him I was practicing riding a lot? Did you tell him I was getting really good? Did you tell him?"

"Yeah." I cleared my throat. "Yes, I saw Kit. And yes, I told him how good you're getting." I swallowed. "He wants to come over and watch you ride."

"Yay! Yay!" Clemmie cried, dancing around me, stepping on me. "Can he come tomorrow?"

"I don't know."

"Can I call him and see? Do you know his number?"

I didn't want Kit to come. Or what I really wanted was for him to come but for no one to know about it. Although it probably didn't matter now that Russ and his big mouth were spreading his cooked-up news. Why had I tried so hard to be friends with Kit when I knew I was asking for this if anybody found out? Then I was angry again. Why shouldn't I be able to be friends with anybody I wanted, not just people Russ thought were OK?

"I do know his number," I said.

Kit told Clemmie he could come the next day. The rain tapered off during the afternoon, and just before sunset, the sky was arced, from the hills in the north to the flatlands in the south, with a vivid double rainbow.

"Do you think there's gold at the bottom of that?" Clemmie asked, pointing.

"No," Dad said. "I think there's mud."

Clemmie's eagerness to see Kit was so noisy and explosive that no one noticed how quiet I was.

He showed up after lunch, by which time Clemmie was practically ready for a rubber room. She ran out into the yard before the wheels on his old Blazer had even stopped turning. She yanked open his door and pulled him by the hand.

"Come *on,* Kit, you have to see me ride. I can make Peaches go real fast, and I can stay on like I'm glued there." She dragged him to the corral, where poor Peaches had been saddled and ready for hours.

Clemmie gave a demonstration of her ability—cantering, trotting, and running Peaches around the corral—while Kit sat on the fence, clapping, giving her thumbs-up, and shouting encouragement. I was afraid she'd hurt herself showing off for Kit, but she really did seem to have improved. Why wouldn't she, with all the practicing she'd done?

When she'd finished, Kit gave her a couple of high fives. "You looked great up on that big horse. You can start with Little Britches rodeo anytime you want to. You'll be a natural barrel racer. But you might want to think about working with another horse. Peaches may be a little old to be starting competition."

"I don't want to be in Little Britches," Clemmie said. "I want to be in the circus. I want to wear some feathers in my hair and a sparkly costume, and ride standing up on my horse."

"Since when?" I asked. "I never heard you say that before."

"Since now," she said. Then she gave Kit a coquettish look from beneath her lashes. "Would you like to be in the circus, too? We could be the horse trainers and the star riders."

"Sounds pretty exciting," Kit said. "But I'm busy going to school to be a vet. Maybe I could be the one who takes care of your horses when you're in the circus."

"I guess that'd be OK," she said. "What shall we do now?"

"How about a video?" Kit said. "I brought one with the Royal Lipizzan stallions I thought you might like to watch."

"The what?" she asked.

We walked to the house while Kit explained, and then, with Clemmie parked, transfixed, in front of the TV, we were alone.

"How come you're so good with kids?" I asked.

"Don't forget, I want my life's work to be with sick, scared animals. Patience is a required course. Anyway, Clemmie's a cute kid."

"The feeling's obviously mutual. I've never seen her flirt with anybody the way she does with you."

"I'm good at flirting with six-year-olds," Kit said. And then his face got serious. "But it's something I've got to be careful about."

"Careful? What do you mean?"

He looked away from me. "There'll always be people who think guys like me...that we're predators or something."

The idea of *anybody* doing *anything* to Clemmie almost made me sick. The idea that someone could think Kit would do that was disgusting.

Kit watched my reaction. "I have to be careful, that's all I'm saying—and most careful around little boys. But I don't think it's a good idea for me to be alone with Clemmie. Then, there's no way anybody can think... well, you know."

I couldn't think of anything to say. Kit's life was a foreign country where all the rules were new to me. He was right when he said a lot about our lives was similar. But where they were different, they were *very* different.

"I'm sorry," Kit said softly. "But that's how it is."

I took a deep breath. "Speaking of how things are, Russ saw me leaving your motor home yesterday. He was driving out of the parking lot just as I left. He'd been there since right after the rodeo, watching."

Kit swore. "That's what *I* call a pervert. And I bet I can guess what he had to say. About you and me."

"Yeah," I said.

Kit turned away from me. "I should have made you leave. I knew I should." His voice was harsh.

So was mine. "I wanted to stay. It wasn't your call or your fault."

Kit made a fist but didn't know what to hit with it. "Why can't I just have my life? What's so unreasonable about wanting that?" He turned around. "What are you going to do?"

"Well, I don't think punching him out will do any good, though that's my first choice. You got any suggestions?"

"Just what I always do—ignore it as much as you can. Deny the parts that aren't true. Fight only if you have to. The difference is, at the end of the summer, I'll go back to State and get out of here. You won't."

"I wish I could."

"That story'll die hard, if it dies at all. You've spent too much time with me. And you don't have a girlfriend. I don't think we should hang out anymore."

That idea made me furious. "Nobody tells me who my friends can be," I said. "Especially not Russ Millard."

"You don't know what you're talking about," he said. "You have no idea."

"Maybe," I said. "So I guess I'll find out." This time I heard my instincts. They were telling me I was throwing away a chance to be protected. I also understood that I might be sorry I hadn't taken it. But I knew I wasn't going to.

We were silent, facing away from each other. Then I turned back to him. "As long as you're here and the damage is done, you want to shoot some hoops?"

He laughed and nodded.

We fooled around with the basketball until Dad came in at the end of the day. He sank a few himself before he asked Kit to stay for dinner.

"Oh, yes," Clemmie said. "Yes, yes, you have to. And you have to sit next to me."

Kit looked at me, shrugged, and said, "All right. But I need to call home first."

He went to use the phone in the kitchen, where Mom, Caroline, and Sally were making lasagna.

"Hi, Kit," Caroline said.

"Hi, Caroline. How's it going?"

"OK. I hear you're doing pretty well at the rodeos."

"Not bad," he said. "I know riding bulls sounds crazy to some, but I think it's fun."

Sally shook her head. "Testosterone poisoning," she said as she set the table.

Kit laughed. "Could be. No doubt in my mind that women have more common sense than guys."

Mom said, "That's a very popular opinion around here. With us females, anyway." I could see Kit's good looks and charm working on those females, effortlessly, naturally, no matter what they knew about him.

"Howdy needs a bath," I said. "Do we have time before dinner?"

"Barely," Mom said. "But he really does need it, so go ahead."

Struggling with a dirty squirming dog was enough to occupy all my thoughts.

As I wielded the hair dryer over Howdy, Kit said, "You'd better be glad Russ can't see you now in this perfect hairdresser moment."

"Well, personally, I think old Russ could do with a razor cut, a deep conditioning, and a few blond streaks around his face." I hadn't spent years listening to four sisters talking for nothing.

Kit burst out laughing.

When we were finished, Howdy, as white and fluffy as a bouquet of dandelion puffs, looked pleased and embarrassed, in equal parts.

Clemmie hugged him. "Oooh, Howdy, you're so

beautiful. You should be in the movies!" With royal dignity, Howdy licked her face.

All through dinner I kept wondering what my parents, my sisters, even Howdy, would say if they knew of the rumor that had already started about Kit and me. I didn't know for sure if anybody had told my dad about Kit, but I doubted it. He was being more relaxed than I suspected he would be if he knew. And maybe Mom was being nice to him the same way she'd have been nice to some handicapped person she didn't know, but I was grateful she wasn't making any kind of a production about having a gay person at the dinner table. I just didn't see how anybody could feel threatened by Kit, but maybe I was naive to think that way. And I had to remember that not so long ago he had made *me* very nervous, too.

Kit and I never had another minute alone because of Clemmie's refusal to leave his side, right up until the time he got into his Blazer to go home. But even if we had, I don't know what else we could have said.

A couple of evenings later, Bobby called. The only time we ever talked on the phone was when we were arranging some time to get together, so I kept waiting for him to get to the point. But he seemed to be beating around some other point until finally it dawned on me what he was hinting at. I wasn't going to help him.

At last he said, "I was at the Dairy Queen last night. There's something going around."

I waited.

Bobby went on after making a few hesitant sounds. "About you."

"Is that right? What?"

"It's about you and Kit."

"Maybe that we're formidable rodeo competitors?"

"No. Not that. That you and Kit are...are...together. If you know what I mean."

"I know what you mean." Then I had one of those moments when I said something and I didn't know why. "And what if we were?"

"Don't put me on," Bobby said. "You're not a fag."

"How about if we don't use that word, OK?"

"Sure," he said agreeably. "So, what are we going to do? How do we convince everybody there's nothing going on with you and Kit?"

Again I went with my instinct, even if I didn't understand what it was doing. "What if there was? Would you care?" I felt like I'd stepped out on a high wire with no net under me.

"Well, jeez," Bobby said. "Sure I'd care. Are you kidding?"

"You didn't care when I was with Kelsey."

"Yeah, but that's different. She's a girl."

"I thought you were OK with Kit being gay."

"Well, yeah. I am. But that's *Kit,* just some guy I know. It's not you."

"You don't think there could be other OK gay guys besides Kit? Ones that Kit might want to be with? Or is he only all right as long as he stays unattached?" I was out on the middle of the high wire now.

"Hey, what is this? You know I like Kit. But to think of him with *you*—practically one of my brothers—no. It's too weird."

"Why is it weird?" I was pushing him, I knew it. But I was pushing myself, too.

"I don't know, man, it's just weird. What are you telling me—that it's *true* what everybody is saying?"

"No," I said, "it's not true."

"Well, then, what's all this discussion about?" Bobby asked. "We need to be deciding what to do."

"How about just ignoring it?" I suggested, though I wasn't sure I could. "Waiting for it to go away?"

"Can you stand that?" he asked, incredulous. "Knowing what everybody's thinking? Wondering if they'll ever stop thinking it?"

"I don't know. I need some time to decide."

"Well, you know I'm with you, buddy. Even if you want to break kneecaps or whatever, I'm with you."

"Thanks, Bobby. I'll let you know."

I went to bed, but I didn't sleep.

By the next afternoon, Howdy was dirty again, and he smelled like his old doggy self. No future for me in the beauty business, apparently.

Clemmie was already plotting another visit with Kit. "I can learn a new trick fast," she said. "And then Kit can come back and see me."

I couldn't tell her that Kit probably wouldn't be coming over again. Being a friend to me had brought him trouble he didn't need. Why would he want to make it worse?

At dinner Clemmie talked about Kit and the Lipizzans, and how he would be the vet for her horses when she was in the circus.

I could hardly listen to her. Her innocent affection for Kit was so uncomplicated, so untainted by what went on in the grown-up world.

One good thing about having four females at a dinner table: You don't have to worry about the conversation. They'll keep it going and not expect you to participate. In fact, sometimes they're irritated if you try to. Often it seems that your presence is enough; you can leave your mind in the garage. And that's where mine was.

I couldn't concoct any plan that would shut up the gossip and still allow Kit and me to stay friends. I knew my life had taken a turn in an unexpected direction, but I didn't know yet if I could get back on the main road or if I was headed off for good.

After dinner the only company I wanted was Howdy's. I'd been neglecting him and I felt guilty. Besides, he asked no questions, expected no explanations. With him I was fine the way I was.

I threw the stick and threw it and threw it, determined that he'd be the one to give up first, not me. It was dark by the time he got tired. And even then I didn't go in. I brushed him, patiently working out all the tangles in his fur. He loved being brushed, and he lay contentedly in my lap, panting, turning from side to side and onto his back as I worked my way around him.

Clemmie came out and sat on the porch step above me. "When are you coming in?" she asked. "I have to go to bed pretty soon, and I wanted you to play a game with me."

"I've got a lot more to do on Howdy," I said, committed to my task. "Ask Caroline or Sally."

"I did. They said no. How come you like Howdy better than me?"

I shut my eyes, then opened them. "I don't," I said. "But I've started this job on him and I want to finish it. I told him I would. He'll be disappointed if I don't."

"He's just a dog," she said, her voice watery with tears. "I'm a real person." As often happened when she got overtired, she became dramatic, easily wounded, quick to weep, and there was no way to head her off. The only solution was to give in to her.

"Oh, OK," I said, sighing. Howdy sat up as soon as I removed the brush from him, as if he knew he'd been outmaneuvered. In the light from the living-room window, his big dark eyes shone with disappointment and dejection. "Sorry, Howdy," I said. "I'll finish you tomorrow."

He uttered a long thin whine as if he were saying I couldn't be trusted to stay his friend through even a small difficulty.

It didn't work out that well with Clemmie, either.

She was too tired to concentrate on the game, but she couldn't stand losing. She started a tantrum that she lost control of and ended up being hauled off to bed, kicking and wailing, by Mom.

I knew how she felt. I hadn't had such a great day myself.

SIXTEEN

MY DAYS DIDN'T GET ANY BETTER. IN THE TWO WEEKS before the state fair, I didn't go anywhere. When Bobby called to see if I wanted to go to town, to hang out at the Dairy Queen, to come over to his place, or to drive to Kit's to practice on the bull, I made excuses. I didn't want to have to see anybody. I suppose I was hiding, though I wouldn't have admitted that then.

Bobby was getting pissed, I could tell.

"What are you afraid of?" he asked. "The more you avoid everybody, the more it looks like that story's true."

He was right. I knew it, but I couldn't make myself do anything about it, and I couldn't explain that to Bobby. He didn't understand a problem that couldn't be fixed by a good fight or a hard ride on a fast horse.

He gave up on me. "OK, be a hermit. When you've had enough of that, you call *me.*"

I didn't call anybody. It seemed easiest to work somewhere alone, sweating and laboring with a shovel or a fence-mending tool or a bunch of cows, or to sit in my room by myself, not reading or watching TV, just sitting.

I even thought, in a remote, abstract sort of way, of running away. I knew I'd never do it, but it helped to think about going to that fantasy place where I could be somebody else. Most of the time I was as baffled as Bobby was at my behavior. I knew that if people hear something for long enough with no argument against it, they'll believe it's true. Why *didn't* I try to help myself?

Trusting your instincts is hard to do when the reason for what they want you to do is so mysterious, but I did it. I had to believe there *was* a reason, and that sooner or later it would become clear to me. The fact that I never believed my lack of action was caused by pure fear was a big help.

I'd pretty much decided I wasn't going to the state fair. I wasn't focused enough to be able to get on a bull without ending up trampled into dog food. And I liked the idea—for the first time in my life—of being all alone on the ranch. Aloneness had its appeal. So much easier than those good old interpersonal relations.

"Are you taking me on the Ferris wheel?" Clemmie asked after lunch. "I'm big enough this year for the Super Wheel. I want you to be the one to take me."

"Maybe you better go with somebody else," I said. "I bet Sally would take you."

"I don't want to go with Sally. I want to go with you."

"The thing is, Clem, I'm not sure I'm going to the fair."

For once in her life, Clemmie was speechless. But not

for long. "You *have* to go. You have to. You have to do the rodeo. You're just kidding with me, right?"

"Well, I'm thinking about not going."

"Well, stop thinking," she said imperiously. "You have to go."

"I'll talk to you about it later, Clemmie, OK?" I said. "I have to go now. Dad needs me to pick up some stuff in town."

"Take me, take me, take me," she begged, jumping up and down, hanging on to my arm.

"Can't," I said.

"Why not? Why not?"

I swear, sometimes I wanted a magic wand that would make her disappear for a while. "Because I can't. There's not room in the truck. I'll be filling it up."

"I won't take up much room. I can make myself *real* small." She squinched herself up into a little ball on the floor, and while she was in that position, I bolted.

Howdy began jumping at me as soon as I was out the door, and I didn't have any choice but to let him bound into the truck ahead of me. Clemmie was at the porch door, yelling after me, "How come Howdy gets to go and I can't?" as I gunned the truck out of the yard.

Howdy was elated—in the *truck,* going for a *ride,* with *me,* all *alone.* Bliss. He hung his head out the window, his front paws on the sill, his ears and tongue flapping.

I knew there was a risk in going to town—a risk of seeing somebody I didn't want to see—but I couldn't say no to Dad without making him ask questions I didn't want to answer. I'd make it quick, stick to business, no stopping by the Dairy Queen, like I would have a month ago, to hang out and see who was doing what. I'd continue my self-imposed isolation even though it was beginning to feel more like torture than refuge.

I parked around the side of the feed store, instead of in front, recognizing that I was hiding and doing it anyway.

"Stay, Howdy. Stay," I told him, and headed inside with my list. I looked back at Howdy watching me go, grinning and panting and wagging the little stump of his tail.

When I finished my shopping, I wheeled the loaded pallet back out to the truck and heaved the bags and boxes from it onto the open bed. I'd take one slow ride through town and then go home, I decided. Make it a test. See if I could find my old self again.

It was a midweek afternoon and so hot the asphalt I drove on was soft. The street was quiet, sleepy, almost without traffic. The blast of sun washed out color and made the main street seem like one in a ghost town. Even the geezers that usually hung out on the benches in the courthouse square had gone someplace cooler.

I was thirsty and lonely. "Want a drink, Howdy?" I asked, giving the decision to him.

He panted.

So I convinced myself the Dairy Queen wasn't such a risky destination at this time of day. I wanted some normalcy for a change. I decided to just do what I felt like doing.

The frigid air-conditioning inside the Dairy Queen made goose bumps pop out on my arms, and the sweat dried along my hairline so fast I expected to find icicles there. No one else was in the place.

"Hey, Johnny." Pam, the counter girl, was a classmate. "Hot out there?" She was wearing a sweater over her uniform.

"Pretty hot," I said. I wondered if she'd heard any of the stuff going around about Kit and me. She must have. But she didn't show it.

"What do you need?" she asked.

"First, a bowl of water for my dog out in the truck."

She filled a plastic ice-cream dish with water and pushed it across the counter to me. "What else?"

"Lemonade," I said. "Extra large. And some fries. Anybody else been in today?" I asked.

She shrugged while she poured my lemonade. "We were busy at lunch. The usual crowd."

I'd just sat down at one of the booths when Russ came in with a couple of his pals. They all had construction jobs for the summer at the shopping center that was going up at the edge of town. They were tan and sweaty and muscular, and full of the swagger that guys get when they spend a lot of time doing things they think of as extramanly. *The way Kit could have been,* I thought, *about bull riding, if he'd been a different kind of person.*

"Well hi, sweetheart," Russ said to me. "All alone? Where's your honey?"

I said nothing. I could have gone straight home from

the feed store, but I hadn't. And maybe this was why I hadn't: to test myself against Russ about this business with Kit.

"Oooh," Russ cooed. "Pouting? Are you mad because I spilled your little secret? I know your sweetie Bobby says there's nothing going on, but you and I know different, don't we?"

He was standing next to my booth, blocking my way out, his hands on his hips, while the other two guys went to the counter to order.

"Such a picture I have in my mind," he went on, "the two of you pretty boys going at it. It must break the hearts of many local girls, knowing they're out of the running with you counterfeit guys. How'd you fool Kelsey for so long? She must be even dumber than I thought."

"Leave Kelsey out of this," I said, determined to keep my cool, to control myself. I wanted to see if I could handle this without a stupid fight.

"Such a gentleman," Russ said. "I wonder how much she'd appreciate being defended by a fag. I know she's with Bobby-dear now, but I'm not sure he's an improvement. The two of you spend a little too much quality time together."

"Leave Bobby out, too," I said.

"Well, I guess that just leaves you and your kitten. How cozy."

"What's your problem?" I asked. I really would have liked to know. Had he just absorbed his father's and grandfather's attitudes without ever letting his own brain get involved?

"You're the one with the problem, buddy. Not me," he said. "Guys like you are an insult to the male race."

"Oh, give it a rest," I said, disgusted, tired of him and his pinched little mind.

"Hey, Russ," one of his pals called from the order counter. "Time's passing. What do you want?"

"Order me a cheeseburger," he called. "I'll be right there."

"So long," I said. "It was a pleasure, as always."

He laughed. "What a shame. You could have made a pretty good guy." He turned to his friends. "Bye, babe," he called to me.

I was sweating in spite of the glacial air-conditioning, and my stomach was so tight I was almost sick. But I'd faced him down and done it to my satisfaction. My fries were too cold to eat, not that I could have swallowed anything then.

I was about to get up to toss them in the trash and head outside with my lemonade and the bowl of water for Howdy when through the front window I saw Kit pull up in his old Blazer. He came in, trailed by a puff of hot air. He saw Russ first and then me. He nodded slightly.

"John," he said.

He was wearing dark glasses, so I couldn't see his expression, but he didn't slow down between the door and the counter.

This was too good an opportunity for Russ to resist.

"Kitten!" he called from where he leaned against the wall, waiting for his burger. "What a nice surprise. Aren't you even going to say hello?"

Kit looked over at Russ and his head dipped slightly. Was he actually nodding at Russ? He turned back to the order counter.

"And what about your sweetie John?" Russ asked. "You don't seem very glad to see him."

Kit ignored Russ. And me. He ordered something— I couldn't hear what—and paid for it. If he was smart, he'd have asked for that order to go.

Russ got up and walked over to Kit. "Hey," he said, "I'm talking to you."

Kit looked at him. "That's true," he said. "It always surprises me that you can do more than grunt."

It took a second for Russ to get it, but then he was really mad. He shoved Kit back against the counter. "Nobody talks to me like that," he said.

Kit didn't say anything.

Without knowing I'd risen, I found myself on my feet. Kit saw and put his hand out, palm toward me, like a traffic cop.

I came at him fast, a red haze behind my eyes. I pushed him. Hard. He stumbled sideways, knocking over a trash can, which spilled all over the floor. Pam stood at the counter, her eyes round and her hands clasped tightly over her apron. Both Kit and Russ looked at me in astonishment.

I was astonished, too, but I couldn't stop. I pushed Kit again, and he fell back over the trash can and sprawled into the spilled garbage, his dark glasses falling off.

"You don't tell me what to do," I said. "I can decide

for myself. Isn't it enough all these lies about me have started because of you?" I stood over him, my fists clenched at my sides. "Get up, so I can hit you again."

"Who could turn down an invitation like that?" Kit asked, not moving.

Russ stood back, watching us, as surprised as I'd ever seen him.

"Get up!" I didn't recognize the sound of my own voice.

What was I doing?

Slowly Kit got to his feet. "I just want to remind you that the lies came from somewhere else, not from me," he said.

"If you weren't what you are, there wouldn't *be* any lies." I went for him once more, but at the last second, my fists unclenched and I ended up pushing him again, my palms on his shoulders. He didn't raise his hands against me. He shuffled backward through the trash, his back hitting the counter. Pam stepped all the way across to the opposite wall. Grabbing him by his shoulders, I shook him. "Why?" I said, anguish in my voice. "Why?" I wasn't even sure what I was asking.

"John," he said. "Stop."

I did. My arms dropped to my sides, and I felt like crying. I couldn't look at Kit. I shook my head and turned for the door.

"Your water," Pam said in a tiny voice.

I stopped where I was. "What?"

"Your water," she said again. "For your dog. Remember?"

I went back for the bowl I'd left on the table and, without looking at Russ or Kit again, left the Dairy Queen.

Howdy was panting like a freight train, even though I'd left the windows of the pickup rolled down. I put the bowl of water on the floor of the cab, and he jumped down off the seat and started lapping messily, dragging his ears in it. I wanted to go, not to be sitting there when anybody else came out.

As soon as the final drops of water had been licked off the sides of the bowl, I slammed the truck in gear and tore out of the parking lot. In the rearview mirror, I saw only dust.

Even taking the long way home, I couldn't bring any order to my thoughts. All I knew was that some corrosive emotion had erupted in me in a completely unexpected way. At least, I wanted to think that it was unexpected. I didn't want to believe that I was capable of attacking Kit just to convince Russ that there was nothing going on between us. How could I do something so low? Was I, who could get on a huge enraged animal with a brain the size of a walnut, really so much of a coward that I would attack an innocent person to cover my own ass?

Clemmie was on me as soon as I got home.

"I told Daddy you didn't want to go to the state fair, and he said you had to, that whatever is ailing you won't be cured by staying at home alone and moping. And he said that Kelsey wasn't the only girl in the world, and that you might even meet somebody nice at the fair. Did you know he and Mommy met at a fair? Is Kelsey why you're so grumpy all the time? Did she say something mean to you?"

I groaned as I unloaded bags of feed.

"Is that heavy?" Clemmie asked. "I can help you." She took the end of one bag and made things even harder by getting in my way.

"Hey," she said, as Howdy jumped out of the truck, the Dairy Queen dish in his mouth. "Did you go to the Dairy Queen with *Howdy*? And you didn't bring me anything? And you took him instead of me to start with?" Tears welled and spilled from her eyes. She dropped her end of the bag and ran into the house.

I stood there, literally holding the bag, feeling as worthless as I ever had in my life.

I got everything unloaded and recognized that I would have to go to the state fair. There wasn't going to be any easy way out. And I deserved the punishment of it.

SEVENTEEN

WE LEFT FOR THE FAIR AT SEVEN IN THE MORNING, with both the van and the pickup. Clemmie went in the truck with me, but fortunately she was so sleepy she just curled up on the seat with her pillow and her blanket and kept quiet. The new silver-belly Stetson I'd shaped so carefully over a steaming teakettle—and looked forward all summer to wearing for the first time at this fair—was in the hat rack on the truck cab's ceiling, mocking my expectations.

The state fair is the biggest deal of all: more rides, more food, more animals, more people, more excitement. It was big enough that I could easily avoid seeing anybody I knew, as long as I stayed away from the rodeo grounds, which I could still do. All I needed was to keep away from my dad, who was determined that the camaraderie of other cowboys and a ride on an angry pot roast, with the possibility of death and dismemberment, were just what I needed to cure my blues, which he was convinced were the result of my split with Kelsey.

As early as we were, the parking lot was almost full: too full for me to tell if there were any vehicles that I recognized.

Colorful flags hung in the still, warm air. We could hear the calliope music coming from the midway and smell the familiar aroma of enclosed farm animals—a smell that would always make me feel safe and at home.

Ralph had come for the weekend, so he and Caro hustled off for a little private fair-time. Mom, Dad, and Sally headed for the home-arts building to leave the pies and Sally's collection. Clemmie and I started across the dirt lot, trailing everyone else. She was so excited, she was skipping. "The Super Wheel first; that's what I want to do."

"I don't know," I said, trying to find my old familiar footing of teasing her. "I think you're still maybe too little for it. You'll slip through the cracks and have to learn to fly in a hurry."

"I am not. I'm exactly big enough. And I could fly if I had to."

As much of a pest as Clemmie could be sometimes, she had something I didn't: the certainty that she was fine just the way she was and the belief that she could do whatever she needed to do.

The second we stepped into the crowded midway, hemmed in on both sides by booths selling Texas dough-nuts and Ginsu knives, water filters and cotton candy, and in spite of my certainty that I could avoid seeing anyone I knew, the first people I spotted were Bobby and Kelsey. They were holding hands.

"Hey!" Clemmie said. "There's Bobby! And Kelsey! Hey, Bobby! Bobby!" she yelled. "Hi!"

Bobby and Kelsey turned. As soon as he saw me, Bobby dropped Kelsey's hand. But she grabbed it right back and held on tight, giving me a defiant look.

"Hi, John," Bobby said, more reserved than he'd ever been with me. He must have heard about the Dairy Queen incident. News like that spread fast through our particular little grapevine.

"Bobby," I said. "Hey, Kelsey."

"Hi, Johnny. Hi, Clementine," Kelsey said.

"So," Bobby said politely, "you ready to ride?"

"Ready as I ever get. How about you?"

We'd never in our lives talked to each other this way—like we were strange dogs, walking stiff-legged and suspicious around each other, ready to bite if we had to.

"Got my lucky new shirt on," he said. It had red, white, and blue diagonal stripes, with white stars on the front and back yokes and red pearlized snaps down the front.

"It's be-yoo-tiful," Clemmie said. "You look like a flag."

"That's the idea," Bobby said. "And the flag's not supposed to be dragged in the dirt, so I'm hoping I won't be, either."

Kelsey hung on to Bobby's arm, rubbing her cheek on his shoulder. "He's going to be sensational today."

"I'm sure he will be," I said, being polite myself.

"We're going on the Super Wheel," Clemmie said, pulling my hand. "I'm not afraid at all."

"That's where we're headed, too," Kelsey said. "I'm not afraid, either."

"We can go together," Clemmie said. "OK?"

What could I say? We walked in silence, Clemmie hanging on to me as tightly as Kelsey was hanging on to Bobby. Dangling in midair on a contraption thrown together in the middle of the night by sleep-deprived carnies was going to seem like a Hawaiian vacation, as long as Clemmie and I weren't in the same compartment with Bobby and Kelsey.

We weren't. At the end of the ride, Clemmie wanted to go again. I was happy to oblige, since I didn't want another awkward stroll with Bobby and Kelsey, trying to think of things to say. From the top of the wheel, I watched them walk away hand in hand. I saw them stop to talk to somebody—could it be Kit?—and then the wheel went down and I lost them.

There were several hours to kill until the rodeo, and it looked like I would be killing them with Clemmie.

By noon I was more than ready to meet my family for lunch and pass Clemmie off to Mom like one of Howdy's well-loved tennis balls.

Ralph and Caro were looking moonily at each other across the picnic table while Mom and Sally laid out the food, ignoring them. Their kind of romance was so commonplace, so ordinary, as to be ignorable. How would Mom and Sally be acting if it was Kit and me? Why would that be so different?

"So, you heading over to the rodeo grounds now?" Dad asked me after lunch.

"I guess," I said.

"Well, don't get *too* enthusiastic," he said sarcastically. "You need to be more pumped up than that if you're going to face off with a bull."

"I'll be pumped up when I need to be," I said, hoping that it was true. Well, maybe I could get kicked in the head and then all my troubles would be over. It didn't sound so bad.

The rodeo grounds were crowded—if you missed every other local rodeo, this was the one you made sure you got to. Yet even as big as the crowds were, I knew avoiding Kit wasn't going to be possible.

I found an area away from the other bull riders, behind a bunch of saddle bronc riders meticulously going over their rigging, to do my stretching and taping and to get psyched. I was having the fantasy that I could stay hidden until it was my turn to ride, then go out, score an impossible one hundred points, win the money, the trophy, and the new saddle, and vanish again, leaving behind people asking, "Who *was* that cowboy?" All except for Kit, who would know, and who would then forgive me for acting like some kind of lunatic. But why should he?

It almost worked out that way—but I just managed

to stay hidden until it was *Kit's* time to ride. And that probably only because nobody was looking for me.

I should have known better, but when I heard the announcer say Kit was up next and then go on about what an up-and-coming young bull rider and rodeo star he was, I couldn't help myself—I had to go watch him ride.

Somehow I managed to squeeze through all the other riders wanting to watch, and I got right up to the rails, where I could look through the slats and see the arena but still be hidden from sight myself.

Kit looked great. Strong and confident and fearless. Watching him made my retreaded heart shrink inside my chest at how I'd treated him.

With that air of calm assurance he had, Kit lowered himself onto the bull and sat there, waiting for the gate to open. The bull looked as crazy as they came, tossing his head around, trying to get a look at Kit through his little red eyes, slamming his body against the sides of the chute, pawing the ground. Kit was undismayed, in that almost hypnotized state of total concentration that is the only way to make yourself do what he was doing.

The gate opened and the bull flew out as if there were a hornet's nest under his tail. He bucked and twisted and shook himself, as if he'd had dynamite for lunch, but Kit stayed on, even though it clearly was no piece of pie, as Clemmie would say.

Without remembering doing it, I climbed to the top of the arena fence so I could see better, and in spite of my vow to remain inconspicuous, I heard myself screaming Kit's name, screaming encouragement.

Just as the eight-second buzzer went off, he saw me, and I could tell his concentration faltered.

At that moment, the bull came down lock-kneed on his two front legs, and the jolt sent Kit flying off his back. I'll always wonder if the surprise of seeing me didn't cause him to momentarily loosen his hold on the bull rope. And I'll always feel responsible for what happened next.

Kit hit the ground hard on his right side and lay there, his hat cast off in the dirt. His eyes were closed, and he made no attempt to roll out of the way or to get up. The way he'd landed, I knew that no number of midriff supports, tail pads, shin guards, or tapings could have protected him.

The bull kicked at him with its hind feet, stirring up clouds of dust, so that I couldn't see what was happening. The bullfighters came rushing in with their brooms and horns, trying to distract the bull and get him away from Kit. I didn't pay any attention to them or to the bull. All I knew was that Kit was down and he wasn't moving.

Through the crowd I could see the ambulance backing up to the arena gate, and two EMTs, a tall guy with a bodybuilder's muscles and a petite blond woman who looked like she should be modeling for the Victoria's Secret catalog, jumping out with a gurney. They got Kit on it and strapped in, and then wheeled him to the ambulance.

It pulled away as the announcer called for a round of applause for the "brave young cowboy who wasn't afraid to ride his hardest. And we'll all be pulling for him. Now let's get ready to cheer for the next bull rider...Russ Millard."

I came up after Russ, so I moved to the chutes in a daze, hardly able to think, oblivious to what Russ was doing. I was climbing into the chute when I heard the announcer say, "Oh, too bad. But let's clap for Russ— that's all the pay he'll be getting today."

I could just as well have been sitting on the back of a carousel horse for all the attention I was paying. My concentration was completely gone and so was my urge toward self-preservation. I really didn't care what happened out there once I was turned loose.

The bull broke out of the chute in a frenzy. By reflex I hung on, but I was as boneless as a pillow. I swung and tilted and moved with the bull, as if I were a part of him. I didn't even hear the eight-second buzzer. Only when the clowns came running out did I realize it was time to dismount, which I did with a minimum of effort, rolling once in the dirt and coming up with my hat, my pretty silver-belly, still on. I'd ridden the best ride of my life without intending to, and I didn't care.

When my score was announced, I knew I'd won, but it seemed to be happening far away to somebody else. My father came running out of the stands to thump me on the back, as excited as I should have been.

"Way to go, son! That was beautiful! You looked like you've been doing that all your life."

Mom and the girls showed up, too, more composed, except for Clemmie, who was jumping up and down, yelling. She was the first one to ask, "Is Kit going to be OK? Is he hurt really bad?"

I knelt down to her. "I hope he's not hurt too much, and I hope he'll be OK."

"Can we go see him?" she asked. "To be sure?"

I looked up at Dad. "I'd like to do that," I said.

"You had enough of the fair?" he asked.

More than enough, I thought. *And then some.* "I have," I said. "What about you, Clemmie?"

"I want to go see Kit," she said. "Can I?"

"We won't stay long," I said to Dad. "We probably can't. But I want to see for myself what's happening."

"OK," Dad said. "Give him my best wishes."

"Mine, too," Caroline said. "Tell him to get well fast."

Neither Sally nor Mom had anything to say on the matter.

Clemmie and I gathered up my gear and stopped at the office to pick up my prizes. I stuck the envelope with the check in it into my shirt pocket without even looking at it, handed Clemmie the box with the belt buckle, tucked the trophy under my arm, and slung the saddle over my shoulder before heading for the parking lot. On the way, I bumped into Bobby and Kelsey again.

"Congratulations," Bobby said. "You looked great out there."

"Thanks," I said.

Clemmie opened the box and showed them the belt buckle. "Wow, look how big it is," she said. "Did you get one, Bobby?"

"A smaller one," he said. "The third-place one." He paused and then said, "Too bad about Kit."

"We're going to the hospital to see him," Clemmie said. "To see if he's OK."

"You are?" Bobby said. "I thought you weren't on... on the best of terms."

"What's he mean?" Clemmie asked, looking up at me, the belt buckle in her hand. "What's 'the best of terms'?"

"Nothing," I said, and looked at Bobby. "You want to go, too?"

He looked down at his boots. "Well, we've got to... you know, the barn dance and all. Tell him hi."

"Sure thing," I said. "Come on, Clemmie."

She pestered me all the way to the pickup about what Bobby had said, but I just kept telling her that Kit and I were friends and that everything was fine. I kept telling her what I wanted to be so.

EIGHTEEN

WHEN WE GOT TO THE HOSPITAL, KIT WAS IN SURgery. I bought Clemmie junk food from the vending machines, and we sat in the waiting room, watching TV. His parents arrived. I introduced Clemmie to them, but they sat apart from us and didn't speak. I wondered if they were puzzling over what I was doing there, imagining some kind of romantic relationship between Kit and me. It wasn't hard to wish that was it rather than the tangle of fascination and betrayal that was the truth.

The doctor came out and told us that Kit had a fractured pelvis, a right leg broken in two places, and assorted bruises, abrasions, and cuts, some of them requiring stitches, from where the bull had thrown him and then stomped him. But he was going to be all right— eventually. And tomorrow he'd be moved to a hospital closer to home. That was all I needed to know. I could leave with an easy mind. I would see him another time when we could talk, just the two of us. I needed to explain my actions to him and to myself. To confess my cowardice and shame. To get it off my chest. And to ask for his understanding and forgiveness.

When we left the hospital, I was surprised to find that it was dark outside. I had no idea how much time had passed since we'd left the rodeo grounds.

The dashboard clock read 9:35, and it was an hour-and-a-half drive back to the ranch. Clemmie and I were so full of chips and chocolate and saturated fats that we didn't want any dinner. She fell asleep while I drove, music from the radio filling the cab, putting me into a kind of alpha state that was broken now and then by the high beams on passing cars driven by people too lazy or too oblivious to turn them down.

I was exhausted in my body and my mind. I turned the radio up. Love songs. Nothing but love songs. Sweet love, raunchy love, love gone bad, love gone ecstatic, extramarital love, extraterrestrial love. But no gay love.

In fact, any of those songs could probably be about gay love, but nobody who listened to them ever thought of that. Maybe love was just love, no matter who was doing it, and if you found it, you should be glad, because it wasn't such an easy thing to find. It certainly hadn't been for me.

I pulled into the yard, turned off the lights, the radio, and the engine, and sat there, Clemmie's head warm and heavy on my thigh.

There was lamplight coming through the living-room window, which was odd; usually by this hour, the whole place was dark and we were supposed to be in our beds, with visions of sugarplums dancing in our heads. But this wasn't a usual night.

I slid out of my seat, went around to the passenger side, and hauled Clemmie out, slinging her over my shoulder. When I started up the porch steps, Howdy, curled up on the doormat, raised his head, his tail vibrating. When he saw it was me, he jumped up. I rubbed his ears with my free hand.

My own little misfit. A curly-haired white toy on a ranch where dirt was the main crop. Not the single-minded kind of working dog that was always welcome, but a fluff ball that had turned out to be as tough, competent, and loyal as any of the other dogs, and with a sense of humor to boot. Or maybe considering him a misfit was the wrong way to think about him. Maybe he was just Howdy and happy to be who and where he was. I knew I was glad he was here. Wasn't that what mattered most?

I held the door open so he could follow me inside.

My father was sitting on the couch alone, with the TV on, peering through his reading glasses at a lapful of paperwork.

"Hi, Dad. How come you're up? Isn't it past your bedtime?"

"I wanted to make sure you two got home OK. How's Kit?"

"He's got some broken bones but he'll be all right."

Dad rubbed his eyes. "That's good. Want me to take Clemmie up?"

"I'll do it. You're working."

He shoved the papers aside. "Not anymore. I was just waiting for you." He stood. "Give her to me."

I handed her over, totally limp deadweight. "I think I'll sit up for a while. I'm kind of wired."

"You've had an exciting day. Where's the trophy?"

"In the truck. The saddle and the buckle, too. The check's here." I tapped my pocket.

"How much?" he asked.

I pulled out the envelope and opened it. "Seven hundred and forty bucks."

"Not bad for eight seconds' work," Dad said. "Too bad you can't do that every day."

"Yeah." I never wanted another day like the day I'd just had.

Dad and Clemmie went upstairs, and I zoned in front of the TV. Maybe I could give Kit my new saddle. Or some of my winnings. And maybe he would throw them in my face if I tried.

I woke—still sitting upright on the couch—with sunshine in the window, Howdy on my lap, and an excited evangelist on the TV screen.

The only clear thought in my head was that I knew I was going to the hospital to see Kit.

I did my chores, showered, and had breakfast by myself. Everybody else had gone to church, letting me sleep off my heavy day. I called to make sure he'd been moved to our local hospital, left a note on the kitchen table, and took off.

Kit was having lunch when I got there: Jell-O, broth,

applesauce. His casts were gleaming white, and his face was bruised and swollen, decorated with the little black cross-hatching of stitches.

"Looks good," I said from the doorway.

He turned to face me. "What are you doing here?"

"I came to see you. See how you are."

"I'm doing fine. Now you better leave before somebody you know sees you talking to me." He was mad, and I couldn't blame him.

I came into the room and sat next to the bed. The curtain was drawn between Kit and his roommate, so I didn't know who was on the other side of it, but it was time for me not to care.

"I was a jerk," I said. "I admit it. I don't know why I acted that way at the Dairy Queen."

"I do," Kit said. "You were afraid. So you knew, for a little while, the way I feel a lot of the time, wondering when something like that might happen. I just never thought it would come from you. I totally misjudged you—and it worries me that I can't trust my own instincts when it comes to picking a friend. It's dangerous."

"You're right, I was afraid," I admitted. "But I'd rather be afraid all the time than feel the way I do now about what I did."

"Fine," Kit said. "Then be afraid." He ate some Jell-O.

"And I want to tell you I'm sorry."

"So you're sorry." He grimaced and changed his position in the bed. "I think you better leave now."

"Don't you feel OK?" I asked, alarmed. I wondered if I should call a nurse.

"No, I don't feel OK. You wouldn't either if you were in my shape. But that's not why I want you to leave. I just don't want to talk to you anymore."

"You mean you don't accept my apology?"

"No. I don't accept it. It's just too damn easy for you to come in here and say you're sorry and then disappear again. That's not friendship."

There was nothing I could say. Because I thought he must be right—that no matter how strong a pull I felt in his direction, I didn't understand enough about what friendship meant.

"Go," Kit said.

I went.

When I got home Ralph had just left and Caroline was moping around. Dad was off checking on fences, and Mom, Clemmie, and Sally had stayed in town for a Disney movie.

"You want to go for a ride?" Caro asked. "I'll go nuts if I have to sit here missing Ralph."

"Sure," I said, feeling about the same way myself.

We saddled Doc and Brownie, and they went off at a walk, going where they felt like going, while Caro and I sat on them like sacks of flour.

"I thought you'd be more set up this morning after your big win yesterday," Caro said to me. "Ralph was very impressed."

What did Ralph know? "My fifteen minutes of fame. It already seems like a long time ago."

"Are you worried about Kit? Is that what's got you down?"

"He'll be all right. It'll take some time, but he'll be fine."

"Come on, little brother. You can talk to me. Is it Kelsey? Are you having regrets now that she's with Bobby?"

"No. No regrets." We rode silently for a while, listening to the clop of the horses' hooves on the dirt. Then I asked, "How did you know Ralph was the one for you and not just one of those other lampshades you've dated?"

"Excuse me?" she said. " 'Lampshades'? '*Other* lampshades'?"

"OK, OK, he's not a lampshade."

"That's better. Well, it's true I've dated a few lampshades, and I can tell you, Ralph is no lampshade."

"So how did you know Ralph the Magnificent was your one and only?"

"Hmm. This sounds like regrets to me."

Fine. Let her think it was regrets. I just wanted an answer.

"Well, let's see," she went on when I didn't speak. "First, there's chemistry. Don't underestimate how important that is. It's there or it's not. You can't fake it, and you can't manufacture it. Then there's sense of humor. He makes me laugh. Then, let's see, he's smart and knows what he wants, and he thinks I'm great, and we can talk about anything, and—I don't know—maybe the timing's right, too. I'm ready. So is he. Does that help?"

"Maybe." I didn't know if it helped or not, because I wasn't entirely clear what I was trying to find out.

"If you don't mind my saying so," Caro went on, "and you know I like Kelsey, so it's nothing bad about her—I never picked up on much chemistry between you two. Of course, I haven't seen you together much, since I've been gone, but I was here at Easter and for a few weekends, and I just didn't sense it. Was that the problem?"

"I...could be. Something was missing, that's for sure."

She turned to me, the brim of her hat shadowing most of her face. "Don't worry. There are lots of other girls. You'll find one. And you've got plenty of time."

"I wish I was going to college this fall. I wish I'd been able to graduate when I should have."

"Senior year goes fast," she said. "It won't be long."

Senior year couldn't go fast enough for me. "Have you ever done something you wished you hadn't? Something you wished you could undo?"

She was quiet, thinking, her face in shadow. Then she said, "Sure. Stuff that seemed really important at the time but doesn't so much now. I wish I hadn't worn that green eye shadow for my graduation picture. I wish I hadn't been impatient with Clemmie so much when she was going through that 'why?' stage." She gave me a quick look. "But nothing as big as breaking up with someone by mistake."

She kept thinking this was about Kelsey. Well, that

was OK with me. If she knew what I'd really done, she wouldn't want to be out riding with me.

Later, when Dad and I were in the barn, I asked him the same question.

"Oh, sure," he said. "I wish I'd bought the Huntleys' place when it was for sale. They had some fine pasturage. I wish I hadn't put all that money into my brother's oil venture, the one that came up dry. I can't think of anything else right off the top of my head, but I'm sure there's more. Why? Have you done something you want to undo? Does it have anything to do with Kelsey?"

Why was everybody so hung up on Kelsey? They were all more interested in her than I was.

"Just wondering, I guess," I said, and clammed up. Let him think what he wanted. What I was learning was that other people's regrets had to do with simple mistakes or judgment errors, not with character flaws the way mine did. My kind of regret couldn't be fixed with a simple apology. What was I supposed to do now?

All I could think of was to go back to the hospital and try again. Maybe if I kept at it, he'd finally believe I meant it.

After supper I drove to town, to the hospital.

Kit was dozing, the TV was on, and his roommate was watching it. He nodded to me when I came in. I nodded back and pulled the curtain between their beds. The sound of the curtain pulling woke Kit, and he looked at me, blinking and confused.

"Hi," I said.

"John? What are you doing here?" He pushed himself up in his bed and then used the controls to raise the head of it.

"I came to tell you again how sorry I am for what I did."

"You didn't need to come back. I believed you the first time."

"I feel so bad about it. I was an idiot."

"Yeah," he said, "you were. And I feel bad about it, too."

Hope rose in me. "I still want to be friends," I told him. "I want to prove to you that I can be a better friend."

"I don't think so," Kit said, without pausing even a minute to think. "You had your chance and you blew it, big time. I can't trust you anymore, and I need to be able to trust a friend."

"I promise you, it'll never happen again." My palms were sweating and I was breathing fast. "Never."

"You're right," he said. "It'll never happen again with me because I won't give you the opportunity. You don't get a second chance for everything just because you want one, you know. So you better not count on it."

He was rubbing my nose in what I'd done, though he didn't seem to be enjoying it the way he could have. Maybe that's what he needed to do before he could forgive me. But I was getting a panicky sort of feeling.

"But I'm promising," I said desperately. "I need you to forgive me."

"And I needed you to be a better friend." He leaned back and closed his eyes, looking weary and sick. "Forgiveness is overrated, I think," he said. "Not everything is forgivable. At least not in my book. I'm not going to change my mind, so you don't need to come back. I have enough other things to take care of."

I sat there dumbfounded. "But—," I began. He couldn't mean he never wanted to see me again. He had to be exaggerating to make his point.

Without opening his eyes, he held up his hand. "Please," he said. "I'm tired and I hurt. And that's on top of all the other stuff my life has dished up for me. I don't need this."

I searched my head for something else to say, some other way to persuade him I meant what I said. I began to understand how Kelsey must have felt that night under the trees at the graduation party.

"It's true that actions speak louder than words," he said, using the control to lower his bed. "Your actions told me about you. I don't need to know anything more. Please go. Please."

So I did. If there'd been any way for me to justify staying, I would have, but I could come up with nothing. Offering him my new saddle seemed seriously beside the point.

I sat in the truck, in the parking lot, with the door half open to catch any breeze. When the evening is cooling after a hot summer day, it's like a gift, unexpected, yet the best thing you could think of. I could think of one thing better—the one thing I knew for sure I wasn't going to get.

Losing Kelsey was nothing compared to losing Kit. Because I had wanted him in my life more than I did her.

I thought back to that day at his place, the day we'd picked the blackberries: how we'd talked and I'd watched the sunlight lie so golden on the muscles of his arms when he moved, picking the berries. How I'd watched that arm on the fence at rodeo school. And how I'd watched the rest of him so much else of the time. Remembering that made me feel warm, filled with a sensation I'd never had before—never for Kelsey, that was certain.

For the first time, with Kit, I'd experienced what Caro called chemistry.

Which had freaked me out so completely, I hadn't been able to admit what it was, and I'd thrown it away with both hands. I'd failed my friend because of my own fear and weakness—a fear and weakness that I knew were still in me.

I slammed the door and threw the truck into gear, peeling out of the parking lot.

Russ's heap was parked outside the Dairy Queen, the way I'd been sure it would be. I was churning inside, hot and ashamed and aching. I thought I could feel the seams on my remodeled heart straining, pulling me into a new way of being.

I knew what I had to do to help myself get there.

I walked up to the table where Russ sat with some of his construction-crew buddies and a couple of girls. As they looked up at me, I swept Russ's burger, fries, and drink off the table into his lap. They all just gaped at me for the few seconds it took Russ to shove his chair back so hard it fell over and to grab me by the front of the shirt with both fists. "Are you crazy?" he asked, as surprised as everybody else.

"Let's take it outside," I said. My heart was banging against my ribs.

Russ didn't answer, just pulled me by the shirt out the door and into the parking lot, where he hit me in the face so hard my ears rang. I fought back enough so I didn't totally disgrace myself, but he was bigger and madder and he wanted more to win. And the more he hit me, the calmer I got.

When he was through, I lay on my side on the asphalt, sore everywhere and bleeding from places I hadn't yet counted. The parking lot was warm against my cheek, and I couldn't think of a good reason to get up. Russ kicked me in the side with the toe of his boot, called me a couple of names, and went back inside. I kept lying there, hurting and wondering vaguely how bad my damage was but relieved somehow at knowing I'd taken the beating Kit should have given me. The beating I'd earned.

For the first time in my life, a fight had satisfied me.

I was still lying in the parking lot when Russ and his pals came out. Russ walked right by me and kept going, but one of the girls stopped.

"Are you all right?" she asked. "Should we call somebody?"

I raised my head. "I'm OK," I said. "I'm just resting."

"Are you sure?"

"I'm sure. But may I suggest that you find a better type of guy to hang around with?" I put my head down again.

"Good idea," she said, and left me.

After a while I pulled myself up and staggered to the pickup. I sat there until I didn't feel dizzy anymore and then started the engine. I didn't look at myself in the rearview mirror. However I looked now would be worse in the morning, and Mom would be flipping out soon enough.

I drove home ten miles under the speed limit, with cars behind me flicking their lights impatiently before they zoomed around me. Tanya Tucker sang "Two Sparrows in a Hurricane" to me on the radio, and I felt like I'd been one of them.

My mind was as beaten up as my body. Everything I knew and felt and understood about myself was different now that I was taking an honest look at it. I at last understood why I had always felt so different—and it had nothing to do with having a patched-up heart, or so many sisters, or with my dad's expectations and my mom's disapproval. It was just how I was. And the certainty, as terrifying and unwelcome as it was, had caused a click in my brain, a settling, that couldn't be rejected.

Contrary to what my sister Marty thought, feeling different all this time was completely unrelated to missing a year of school because of heart surgery. My heart could, in fact, perform the trick I'd thought impossible for it: It had fallen in love. Without my permission and without my acknowledgment. It had been more open and astute than the rest of me, which was just now catching on.

It told me that Kit was the first, but he wouldn't be the last. He'd been right—not everybody knew by the time they were seven. And what I already knew about myself—that surrender was more difficult for me than control—was still true. Now I would have to learn how to live this new way without Kit's help and companionship, and it was my own fault.

NINETEEN

THE REST OF THE SUMMER PASSED IN A STEW OF HOT weather and hard work and isolation. I lived so deeply inside my personal turmoil that, even now, I can barely recall anything from that time except insomnia and constant anxiety. It took awhile, but eventually everybody noticed that something was going on with me.

"Johnny," Caro said, after one of her hour-long phone conversations with Ralph, "it's not healthy the way you keep moping about Kelsey. You haven't done anything with Bobby in ages. You never even go to town anymore unless you have to run errands. You need to get your social life started again. Your senior year is coming up. It's supposed to be the best one."

"Yeah," I said. "I know. Don't worry about me. I'll be OK."

How could I say that? All I was thinking was, *How can I ever tell her?* If she knew, could the easiness between us ever be the same again?

But it already wasn't. What I was holding to myself had put up a barrier. We both felt it, but only I knew the reason.

"John," my father said, "you know I appreciate all the help you've been around here lately—all the things you've done without being asked, and all the extra hours you've put in. But you're living like an old man—all work and no play. You need to go hang out with Bobby. Or maybe go see how Kit's doing. I can't say I was happy to hear what your mother told me about him, but he's still a hell of a bull rider, and that's nothing to sneeze at. Even a couple of little fights wouldn't be completely out of line. Just try to avoid one like the last one."

Even Dad had been disturbed by the way I looked after Russ was through with me.

"I will, Dad," I said. "You're right."

So I started taking off in the truck every now and then, staying gone for hours, just driving or sitting on a side road somewhere, terrified and desperate. The something big that I'd anticipated for so long had arrived in the form of a curse, and I didn't know how to break it. I couldn't go backward, not with what I now understood about myself; nor was I able to go ahead. I hung in a miserable limbo, afraid to do anything for fear of giving away my shocking secret.

I sat under a lot of dusty trees, hot even in the shade, and thought about how important it was for my dad to have a son. Could he accept a new concept of what a son was? Could *I*? Could I ever give him the chance? I just didn't see how. And what about Mom, with her ideas of how things were supposed to be, of what was decent and what wasn't? My news would put a serious dent in those. All her concerns about my turning out wrong would be realized in spades. And Clemmie—would she hate me?

Mom took to watching me. I felt her eyes on me in a way they hadn't been for a long time—since I'd had my surgery. She came into the yard one afternoon when I was there alone, sweating over changing the oil in the pickup and the van.

"John," she said.

"What?" I asked, alarmed at the seriousness of her voice. Had she figured something out? I stood up and wiped my hands on a rag.

"I want to say something to you," she said, her hands in the back pockets of her jeans. I braced myself. "I want to tell you how pleased I am at your behavior lately. You've done what you're supposed to and more, according to your father. You've stayed out of trouble. You've thought better of that friendship with Kit Crowe. And you've been so nice and quiet and easy to have around— I have to believe that you're finally growing up. I just want you to know I've noticed."

I kept rubbing my hands on the rag and almost laughed. All it took for her to finally be satisfied with me was for my entire life to be turned so completely upside down that I didn't make sense to myself anymore. Yet she'd be staggered if she knew why she was so pleased with me.

———

Kit, of course, never called. I almost called him several times but stopped with my hand on the receiver. What more could I say to him?

How did he do it? No wonder he could ride bulls with such ease. That was nothing compared to how he lived every ordinary day. Why couldn't you go to a school to learn how to do that, the way you could go to rodeo school or computer school or brain-surgery school? None of that could be as hard as what Kit had done. And what I knew I had ahead of me.

And then there was school. It would be starting soon, and I wasn't the person I'd been in June. Even if Russ's dirt about Kit and me had died out, I was different. And what if it hadn't died out?

I lay in bed at night, restless and sweaty, swarmed by questions without answers.

The night before school started, the house was in an uproar. Caro—who had a week before she had to be back at school—and Mom were helping Sally and Clemmie put together their outfits for the first day. This required many complicated conversations, a few tears from Clemmie, and even a phone call to Marty, who, as always, was happy to give advice. Dad went off to pay bills behind a closed door, and I wished I could be teleported to some distant sister-free planet.

With everyone else so thoroughly occupied, I found myself doing the one thing I thought I'd never do: punching Kit's number into the phone. As soon as I'd done it, I prayed he wouldn't answer. But I didn't hang up.

"Hello?" he said.

My breath choked in my throat, and I was speechless. The sound of his voice brought back everything—those corral-fence conversations in the middle of the night at rodeo school, the splendid spectacle of him riding a big bull, the rainy evening in his father's motor home, the new kind of friendship I had begun to form with him—as well as the afternoon at the Dairy Queen. I couldn't erase that from my memory banks, no matter how much I willed it. Or the hospital visits that brought everything to an end.

"Hello?" he said again.

"Kit?" I managed to say.

"Yeah. Who's this?"

"It's...it's John. John Ritchie."

There was a silence, and I was afraid he was going to hang up.

Finally he said, "Yes?"

"I just wanted—" I had to stop and take in more air. I started again. "I just wanted to see how you are."

"I'm fine. Thanks." His voice was wary, waiting.

"Are you out of the cast?" That seemed safe enough.

"Not yet. After I go back to school."

"So, you're going?" Well, why wouldn't he? I was asking dumb questions only to avoid silence.

"Sure." He waited again.

I didn't want him to hang up, so I rushed on. "I...I wanted to say thank you."

"For what?"

"I learned a lot this summer. From you. I wanted to say thank you."

"Well. You're welcome." He hesitated, and I knew he was trying to decide if he wanted to ask me what I was talking about. He decided. "Good of you to call," he said, and broke the connection.

I sat there, looking at the phone in my hand, knowing that I'd never speak to Kit again but that I'd never forget him. I put the phone back in its cradle and took a deep breath of air already spiced with the scents of fall.

I imagined myself entering the gate to a bucking chute, one that held a giant bull who hated the world. I was going to have to get on board, with my glove tied and rosined, and do my best to stay up on the rope, to keep my chest high, my arm raised, to last my eight seconds. And then there would be eight more. And eight more, and eight more, forever. Some of that time I would be riding well, and sometimes I wouldn't—or as Tyler Thompson would say, I could be a rooster on Tuesday and a feather duster on Wednesday.

And while I rode I'd be remembering Kit, who taught me just how much I wanted more Tuesdays than Wednesdays.